CW01024002

A Wander Through the Village

The Greek Village Handbook

The Eastern Fly and Other Stories

Sara Alexi is the author of the Greek Village Series.

She divides her time between England and a small village in Greece.

http://www.saraalexi.com

http://facebook.com/authorsaraalexi

Sara Alexi

A WANDER THROUGH THE VILLAGE

oneiro

Published by Oneiro Press 2016

ISBN-13: 978-1533024213

ISBN-10: 1533024219

With thanks to everyone who helped on this project…

Dena Patrick, Toni Thomas and Gillian Frost - The Illegal Gardener

Carole Fripp and Gayle Dix Hopkins- Black Butterflies

Susan Yowell and Susan Brown - The Explosive nature of Friendship

June Shirlene Spoonamore – The Gypsy's Dream

Christine Hinton and David Horning - The Art of Becoming Homeless

Jeffrey Efremis Sofroniou and Sharon Scott - In The Shade of The Monkey Puzzle Tree

Susan Brown and Susan Peters - A Handful of Pebbles

Toni Thomas, Juana Abbene and Shauna Brown - The Unquiet Mind

Karen Willson and Anna Marie Baker - Watching The Wind Blow

Gillian Frost and Alexandra Mcternan - The Reluctant Baker

David John Willmore and Anne Whiting - The English Lesson

Marilyn Louise Hillyard and Margaret Baines - The Priest's Well

Catherine Helen Carr and Carol Woodfin- A Song Amongst the Orange Trees

Al Stokes and Mick Dixon - The Stolen Book

Introduction

April 2016

'The Accidental Story Teller.' May not be the best title for book, which is perhaps why, to date, no such work is listed anywhere, at least not if a quick search on the internet can be relied upon.

But if I were ever to write about my experiences as a writer, apart from being very short and full of spelling mistakes, this might be the title of my book. I never intended to write. I am dyslexic, so why would I humiliate myself in this way? But then, one day, something outside of seemed suddenly more important than my ability, or lack thereof. The overwhelming impulse to put pen to paper – or rather, finger to keyboard – manifested itself in the form of a Pakistani illegal immigrant who was weeding the lane opposite my neighbour's house. This was years before the current refugee crisis in Europe. Then, displaced people were not seen as asylum seekers or refugees. They were all just illegal immigrants. This man pulling at the weeds by the road side did not know if he would get paid or even if he would eat that day. He hoped that one day he would have enough money to attempt the journey home to his wife and children. There were many men like him living in and around the small Greek village I had the good fortune to call home.

His story needed telling and there was no-one willing to do the job but me.

As coincidence would have it in less than two months I would hit the ripe young age of fifty. As one hundred seems a reasonable target to aim for, this made my birthday a half way mark and so it seemed only natural to mark this occasion with something I have never done before, something I never ever dreamed I would ever do, something that felt so constructive or ambitious. I would write a book - this book. The story of this man, who was one of so many at the time, and now is one of a sea of faces that come every day from Turkey on inadequate rubber boats packed to the gunwales.

So that was the catalyst for the first book, and I wrote the first draft in about a month. The Illegal Gardener was (self) published on my fiftieth birthday, and I stayed glued to my computer screen the day it was released, waiting. All I wanted was one sale, to know that one person sat somewhere in the world reading what I had written. No sales were recorded but I went to bed still with some hope. Maybe tomorrow someone would buy the book.

I awoke the next day to find I had made 300 sales and the emails were flooding in, demanding that I write a sequel. So I wrote a second book and made it slightly more humorous, as the protagonist dictated. This too was met with a response I never expected and it was suddenly within my grasp to make a full time living as a - and here I hesitate to use the word. I do not feel I can call myself a writer as I don't know what phrases like 'past participle' mean, and proper authors are the likes of Thomas Hardy and Anthony Trollope. I feel a lot more comfortable with the term story teller instead, which conjures up images of folklore, tales by the fireside, gossip that has been adopted as truth.

When the third book was published I realised I had a series all set in and around a Greek village and so The Greek Village Series or Collection was born and the stories popped into my head thick and fast. But now, of course, there are 17 books and I am finding it is very difficult to keep everyones' names in my head, even though I am the one who wrote them! So, as an aide-memoire, and as much for my sake as for yours, I present this handbook.

It is designed so you can look up a book and see who is in it, or look up a name and see which books they appeared in, or were mentioned in.

I have included a map of the village and also one of Orino Island in relation to Saros and the village.

I could not resist including some views of my favourite parts of Greece, and how would any book with the words 'Greek Village' in the title be complete without at least a few stories, letting you catch up with characters you know as well as introducing some new ones.

Sara

Spoiler Alert!

In the pages that follow, there is information about the characters that appear in the first fifteen Greek Village Collection books, and about how they relate to one another.

If you haven't read the books and don't want to spoil the endings, you may prefer not to read on...

You have been warned!

The Greek Village

The Greek Village in the books is loosely modelled on the village where I live in the Peloponnese, but it could be any one of hundreds of farming villages that are scattered all over Greece. There's nothing remarkable about it, but at the same time it has its own unique charm and character.

There's a square and a church, and a *kafenio* where the old farmers sit and while away their time, away from their wives' mops and brooms. There is a little wooden kiosk in the square, selling cigarettes, sweets, drinks and ice creams, and hundreds of other sundry items. Across from the kiosk is a corner shop stocked with all the staples: rice, pasta, vegetables, newspapers, plastic bottles of local wine, eggs still warm from the chicken, shepherds' crooks... The list is endless.

Some days the pharmacy is open; often it is not. The bakery on the other hand is reliable, but you have to be quick - they run out by 10 in the morning!

The church bells wake me at 7 every Sunday with their loud clanging, and at other times they are muted - announcing a funeral.

Cockerels crow at all hours of the day, and dogs bark to one another across the village spasmodically during the day and then in chorus as the night falls. I can hear no noise of traffic from my house, just the goats bells as they are driven out to graze and back again. At night it is as silent as the grave. I've never had a better night's sleep anywhere.

In the daytime, in summer, the cicadas are deafening.

The village is not far from the sea, but I cannot actually see the water from the house. There's a hill in the way, with a dense clump of pine trees on top, and this hill often calls to me, to go walking along the narrow tracks that wind through the countryside.

These tracks take me between orange orchards and olive groves, and out onto barren scrubby land that is designated 'forestry' land, and which cannot be cultivated or built on.

Greece is a mountainous country, and great for hiking. There are few (if any!?) official paths, but no one seems to mind if I accidentally stray across their field or orchard. They are more likely to give me an orange than to tell me to clear off.

In contrast with the UK, for example, wild flowers grow in abundance in Greece. I think this has to do with the levels of pesticides in the UK. In any case, the countryside in Greece is teeming with bold red anemones, shocking purple wild irises, delicate poppies, and daisies by the dozen, as well as tiny orchids hidden away under the bushes.

Bees buzz around these, and crickets fly up from the long grasses. Lizards scuttle across the path in front of me, and occasionally a tortoise will lumber into view. Birds of prey circle silently overhead, and there's nowhere nicer to be in the world!

But my stomach tells me it's time for lunch, and so, reluctantly, I head for home.

The vegetables here are so ripe and full of flavour! I'll chop tomatoes that I bought at the farmer's market yesterday, and fresh spring onions, and crumble in a little feta.

My neighbour gave me a tin of olive oil from her trees last year, and it's still more than half full. I'll drizzle that over, and sprinkle a little oregano from the plant that grows by my gate, and eat my salad with fresh crusty bread and a glass of local wine in the shade of the grape vines - heaven!

The afternoon is a delicate and delightful mix of snoozing and writing in the heat. I lounge on my bed and the hours fly by and the evening comes too soon. Not that there is a rush to do anything in the evening, and it is nice to see friends or head out to a taverna for a meal. But if I am at a point in the latest story that is particularly engrossing I'll just move from the bed to the sagging sofa on the patio and carry on writing.

The Books

The Illegal Gardener

It seems to me that the subject for each book I write comes to me, rather than me going out to look for ideas. I think this first story will always be special to me as it took me from the world of imaginary limitations due to my dyslexia, to being a full time writer, or to be more accurately, a story teller.

Are you sitting comfortably? Then I'll begin. …

As you will probably know if you follow the news, Greece has faced tough times recently, both politically and economically, and the Greek people have suffered financially. In 2012 they responded with demonstrations in the centre of Athens and the images were flashed around the world. Back then I was helping people rent out their holiday homes, and the effects these pictures of the riots had on the tourist industry was catastrophic. I found myself at the age of 49 with no income, and nothing much to add to my resume for the past seven years.

So there I was, bemoaning my lot, thinking how awful my life was. Poor, poor me.

I leaned on the window sill looking at the sunshine, wondering what the downturn in the economy was going to mean to me personally, and there in the heat of the day, down the narrow lane that leads to my house, was a man, squatting, pulling weeds for a neighbour. He looked Indian or Pakistani.

So I wandered out to where he was working and chatted to him, asked him about his life. Anyone who knows me will tell you that I speak to everyone I meet, much to my daughter's embarrassment! This man's English was not good and mostly he supplied one word answers. But it was clear that there was little work to be had. If he got work he would be paid between five and twenty euros a day, he told me. Sometimes food was provided, but mostly not. He had been in Greece for two years but his aim was to get to Spain where he had been told it was easy to get papers that would make him legal, and where there was more work.

We talked more. He had a wife and two children, one of whom he had not yet seen as he left when his wife was pregnant. He had no idea how or when he would return to her. He only earned enough to eat, if he was lucky.

There were another ten such men in the small village, he said.

I was fuming. Purely by the circumstances of our births his life had taken one course, and mine another. The lottery of where we were born defined our whole existence because man, in his wisdom, had placed invisible borders and created random laws to stop people like Aaman from working where they chose.

My anger drove my passion and my passion said this man's tale must be told. So I gave the outline to a writer I knew and he replied 'You write it.' and passed it back. It didn't need saying twice. I was so angry on this Pakistani man's behalf, and on behalf of all the others like him, that I wrote the book. It took me just over a month and was published on my 50th birthday.

I prayed that one copy would sell.

It sold over 300 on the first day.

The Greek Village series that it gave birth to has sold over 700,000 copies at time of writing. (March 2016) and there are still more stories waiting to be told!

Cast of Characters – Illegal Gardener

Juliet – An English woman who bought a house in the Greek village to renovate after her marriage break-up from Mike. Her soul originally lodged in Greece when taking a rejuvenating holiday with her best friend Michelle, leaving her husband and mother-in-law to look after her newly born twins. She is fluent in Greek and works as a translator.

Terrance – Juliet's son, Thomas's twin. Studying waste management at university.

Thomas – Juliet's son , Terrance's twin. In banking.

Cheri – Thomas's girlfriend. Also in banking.

Emily – Juliet's teddy bear when she was little.

Michelle – Juliet's friend from childhood, a lawyer in London.

Richard – Michelle's husband, also a lawyer in London.

Jenny – Juliet's best friend at university.

Mick – Juliet's ex husband, no defined job.

Dr John Brooks – Juliet's college tutor / lover.

Aaman – A Pakistani man who travelled to Greece illegally and ended up living in the Greek village, looking for causal labour.

Saabira – Aaman's wife, lives in a small village outside Sialkot, in Pakistan.

Giaan – Aaman's elder brother, died in a fire aged eight.

Harpeet – Pakistani man who turns up at Juliet's house right at the end of the story.

Mahmout – A Pakistani man living in the village. He tries to befriend Aaman.

Marina – A Greek woman who runs the village shop.

Mitsos – A farmer in the village.

Mrs Eleni – A woman in Marina's shop.

Mrs Sophia – A villager, friend of Marina.

Old Costas – A farmer. Owns the barn where Aaman and the other illegals stay.

Spiros – Naughty boy at the church at the Easter celebrations.

Vasso – Little girl at the church at the Easter celebrations – Spiros' sister.

Vasiliki, often shortened to **Vasso** – Kiosk owner in the village square.

Book Club Questions - The Illegal Gardener

+ What do you think Juliet was hoping for when she left her life behind and moved to a new country?

+ Do you think Aaman went with realistic views, or did he ignore what he thought might be the truth to please Saabira?

+ Why do you think Juliet was angry with Aaman?

+ Why do you think Aaman left the shoes and clothes Juliet offered him all over the patio?

+ Which do you think held Aaman back more, his height or the death of his brother?

+ In what way do you think Juliet helped Aaman emotionally?

+ In what way do you think Aaman helped Juliet emotionally?

+ If things had been different do you think Aaman and Juliet would have made better siblings or lovers?

+ Since the writing of this book (2012) the influx of refugees and immigrants to Europe has reached unprecedented levels. Has reading Aaman's story affected your view of the crisis?

+ If the circumstances arose would you give someone like Aaman a temporary home to help them in their lives as Juliet did?

Black Butterflies

No sooner was The Illegal Gardener published than a conversation with one of my neighbours revealed that she was married at thirteen and had her first child aged fourteen. She took this in her stride, but it made an impression on me.

I was having coffee with a group of my neighbours some days later, and I asked if any of them had married for love, at which this cluster of women in their black skirts and blouses fell about laughing, and when they regained control, one of my neighbours explained, 'It's like being given a pig in a sack. You know that it will be a pig, but you don't know what kind of pig it is until the sack is opened,' and they all laughed out loud again. The woman who related this had been married for forty five years and her husband had recently died, and a sadder widow I have yet to meet.

'Yes!" they all agreed, laughing. 'A pig in a sack.'

'And what of love?' I asked

'Well, there was one boy just before I married,' the first neighbour said, and it was the look in her eye that inspired the story of Black Butterflies, which came to me complete.

I talked for a while longer with this group of women and found out many other things about how they thought, all of which came from the circumstances of their upbringing and education, as it is with us all. We touched on various topics but at one point homosexuality was mentioned and frosty glances betrayed their disapproval. Greek orthodoxy does not approve of or even recognise such things.

'Oh, except for Panos,' one of the women said, and the ice melted and they agreed.

'Oh yes, Panos. Although he is a homosexual you cannot take exception to Panos.' Another replied.

'Nor Katerina and Mitza.' This comment brought more noises of agreement. 'No, you could not include them either,' they agreed, and so it was that the subplot presented itself.

Most of Black Butterflies is set on Orino Island which is a fictitious place based on the real island of Hydra. Here the donkeys are the workforce and once out of the narrow streets of the town you often find donkey manure on the paths. The black butterflies of the island are drawn to fresh piles of donkey droppings and it is here that they gather and settle. It seemed like the obvious title for such a book because, like in the story, from things that we consider nothing but a pile of manure beautiful things can blossom and grow.

Cast of Characters – Black Butterflies

Marina – The protagonist. A woman from the village who runs the village shop. For years she has enjoyed the people coming into the shop and not really going anywhere herself very much. She is appreciative of life and moves at a slow pace.

Meli – Marina's first boyfriend. Meli literally means 'honey', and it is the nickname Marina gave him.

Melissa – literally translates as 'honey bee'. Meli's term of endearment for Marina.

Manolis – Marina's husband

Mitsos – Manolis' childhood friend.

Artemis – Marina's younger daughter. Married and living in Athens.

Eleni – Marina's eldest daughter.

Katerina – Eleni's first girlfriend, at school.

Anna – Eleni's girlfriend. Eleni is Marina's daughter.

Petta (Petalouda) – Marina's son. Real name Alexandros Mavromatis . Petalouda means butterfly.

Irini – Petta's partner / fiancé.

Vasso Mavromati – Petta's step mother.

Costas – A young man who helps out in Marina's shop.

Aunt Efi – Marina's aunt, who accompanied Marina to Orino when she was a teenager.

Kyria Zoe – Runs a pension on Orino island.

Roula – Kyria Zoe's daughter.

Aunt Eleftheria – Relative of Kyria Zoe.

Kyria Zoe's mother – Also referred to as Grandma by Roula.

Bobby – Kyria Zoe's brother in law.

Gypsies – Sold rugs from their truck, and were conned by Manolis.

Kyria Sophia – Marina's next door neighbor in the village. Helps out in the shop.

Malakopoulos – A family from the village who keep goats.

Aris Karnidiotis – Jeweller on Orino island.

Costas Voulgaris – Café owner on Orino island.

Maria – Candle maker on Orino island.

Panos – Hairdresser on Orino island.

Socrates Rappas – Priest on Orino island.

Yanni – Donkey man on Orino island. Known as Black Yanni because of his permanent suntan.

Spiros – One of the port police men.

Stamos – One of the port police men.

Vasilis – One of the port police men.

Petros - Taxi boat man.

Bill and his wife (not named) – American tourists.

Anna Vissi – A well known Greek singer.

Vangelis – Well known Greek composer. Wrote the soundtrack to the film Chariots of Fire

Book Club Questions – Black Butterflies

+ Do you think Marina was scared to go to the island because of her memories or because she was so used to being within her comfort zone?

+ Do you think Marina wanted to return to the island for reasons other than protecting her daughter?

+ Did Irini become a surrogate daughter for Marina and in what ways was this useful for her?

+ Do you think Aunt Efi was in any way to blame for what happened?

+ Marina meets both charming Costas Voulgaris, the globetrotting kafenio owner, and Bobby, Zoe's brother in law. Did you feel she was more comfortable with one of them than the other? If so why?

+ Do you think it helped Marina to see the house she lived in when she stayed on Orino as a child? In what way?

+ What do you think Marina learnt about love, life and about herself when she realised Panos was gay?

+ How do you think Marina's relationship with her husband affected how she saw herself in the world?

+ Do you think Marina had an ulterior, psychological motive in inviting the whole village in to see her husband's private hoard, that she turned into the corner shop?

+ Do you think Marina was ready to meet Petta and this was her true reason for going to the island?

The Explosive Nature of Friendship

A pet hate of mine inspired me to write The Explosive Nature of friendship: the way we treat older people! The older generation have so much knowledge and so much wisdom and yet in Western society we do not hold them in high esteem, and we do not seem to value the experiences they have accumulated through life. We also tend to view them, even (or especially) when they are relations of ours as an inconvenience and we build homes for them and pay others to take care of them.

We say that modern psychotherapy is a new 'science', often dated to the opening of the first psychological clinic by Wilhelm Wundt in 1879.

We have always had philosophers and thinkers and human nature has always been a good topic for discourse. But the idea of therapy, and going to see someone and working through all your issues, would that have come about at all had the extended family remained intact? I am not a historian but at a guess I imagine that the Industrial revolution (1760 - 1840) displaced a lot of the younger generation as they sought work in towns far from where they were born and where their families lived. I do not consider it a coincidence that peoples' interest in psychology flourished such a short time later.

These days very few teenage children would turn to their parents for help or advice, but Granny, dear, sweet, old, knowledgeable Granny will not only give you a bit of her advice but she will crack the odd joke about how silly your mother was when she was a girl too and you are not left feeling that you are the only one. Mum did it all before you and she made a mess of things too. What a relief that must be to hear.

But if granny is dumped in the Sunshine Home for the elderly we have to trot along and pay someone, sometimes even younger than we are, to sit and listen, like Granny would have loved to have done. What a waste of experience and wisdom, accumulated over a lifetime!

As you can see, I get pretty warmed up over this topic.

Another idea I wanted to explore was this: *what if you give a mature person the power to really make a difference in peoples' lives, say, with a big lump of money*. I know how the young would spend it, but how would someone with more wisdom, more years on this planet use such a sum?

'Carefully' was the single word answer I came up with and so Mitsos, as a character, took on his own life.

Cast of Characters – The Explosive Nature of Friendship

Mitsos – The protagonist. A villager, whose life we follow as he grows from a young boy to an old man. He is harsh on himself and thinks his life has amounted to nothing but now, in his old age, he has an opportunity that he think might rectify the wrongs he perceives he has done.

Mr Dimitri – Mitsos' father

Mimi – The family donkey

Manolis – Mitsos' school friend, and the antagonist in the book. He is always up to no good.

Marina – Manolis' wife, who was the protagonist on book 2 Black Butterflies.

Eleni – Marina's elder daughter

Old Costas – Manolis' father. Owned the barn where the illegals stayed

Adonis – Mitsos younger brother

Leni – Adonis' wife

Zorbas – Leni's grandfather

Theo – Manolis' and Mitsos' school friend. Later runs the kafeneio in the village.

Aaman – Pakistani illegal immigrant. Restores Juliet's garden.

Anna – Girl in the travel agent's in Saros town

Aris & Katerina – A couple in the village, who met as a consequence of one of Mitsos and Manolis schemes. Aris mends tractors, and they have ten children

Cosmo – The village postman, and school friend of Mitsos and Manolis

Despina – A kind old lady in the village

Juliet – English woman who moved to the village and is renovating an old farm house. The protagonist in The Illegal Gardener.

Mr Froutokleftis – A fruit buyer who bought from the local farmers but never paid. 'Froutokleftis' translates literally as 'Fruit Thief'

Mr Pseftico – Mitsos' bank manager. 'Pseftico' translates literally as 'False'.

Mr Socrates – Grumpy man who owns the mandarin orchard by the riverbed.

Stella – Runs the eatery / ouzeri in the village.

Stavros – Stella's husband.

Vasso – Runs the kiosk in the village.

<u>Widow Katerina</u> – Village busybody who organized supplies of food for Marina and Mitsos when they were incapacitated after the storm.

Book Club Questions - The Explosive Nature of Friendship

+ Do you think Mitsos's disability is the only reason he shies away from looking after his nephew?

+ What did Mitsos gain by fallowing Manolis's plans?

+ Do you think Mitsos's love for Marina was built on anything real?

+ At what point do you think Mitsos should have told Manolis that enough was enough?

+ Why do you think Manolis was as he was? What factors influenced his character?

+ Do you think that with the right guidance Manolis could have turned his energy into something positive?

+ Should Mitsos have bailed Manolis out of jail or was it better to leave him inside - to reflect?

+ What is meant by the eye contact as Manolis uses his body to take the majority of the impact of the explosion?

+ Do you think Mitsos love for Stella is built on something real?

+ Did he make the right decision about what to do with his windfall?

The Gypsy's Dream

The Gypsy's Dream explores another issue close to my heart: abusive relationships.

This is always a situation where the weak is preyed on by the strong, physically or mentally. This story is about Stella as she struggles to decide whether she can leave her domineering bully of a husband, Stavros, and if so, how.

As with all the books, I am interested in understanding the psychology that draws people into choosing what often does not look like the most rational route. Women who stay in abusive relationships, when it is clear to those who are not involved that they would be better off leaving, are often viewed with amazement. We wonder why they on earth they stay with men who clearly do not appreciate or care for them. The reasons are complex of course, and may include social pressures, feelings of failure, and other factors, and each situation is unique, although it seems that there are often parallels between different cases.

In Stella's case it was only when she witnessed Stavros mistreating Abbie that she finally took the decisive action to leave the relationship. This is something I have witnessed more than once when I was practising as a psychotherapist – a woman might stay in a toxic or abusive relationship as long as she is the only one being mistreated, but if the abuse begins to affect her children, for example, she might make the decision to leave.

This behaviour calls into question the value that a woman (or a man, as of course not all abusive relationships involve the woman being abused) places on her own comfort compared to that of others, and I believe it is this lack of self worth that might be the key in many relationships, and certainly was a part of what made Stella stay as long as she did. At school she was teased because her mother was a gypsy, and she would doubtless have grown up believing that there was something wrong with her heritage. I in fact use Stella's gypsy descent almost as a metaphor for lack of self worth to clearly show how the abuser can hold leverage over the abused without taking any clear action; how the abuser can get 'inside' the victim's mind.

It is only when Stella is in the cupcake shop in Saros town, and a customer makes a positive comment about the gypsy music, that she considers that maybe being a gypsy is not all negative, that indeed there might be something positive in her heritage seeing as this unsolicited comment was said with so much joy.

But I have tried to push it even further forward by taking Stella to the point where she almost transcends everything she has been led to believe and develops a stronger sense of self, emerging with her own identity that doesn't need to rely on labels such as 'Gypsy' or 'Greek'.

Stella's dream has always been to run a successful business (And maybe this too is a metaphor for being an 'independent classless, cosmopolitan woman', and through the power of self belief and with the support of a few good friends, she finds the self confidence to become all she can be. Whether the actual business succeeds or not is almost unimportant, as we all know that if her first venture failed, she would pick herself up and try again.

I don't know if I have managed to put this message across skillfully in the book, but if Stella's tale helps just one person who is in a similar situation to hers, or even gives just one person hope that things can change, then I will feel that the book was more than worth writing.

Cast of Characters – The Gypsy's Dream

Abby – An English girl who travels to Greece and ends up in the wrong town. With little money to get to her intended destination, and a storm that thwarts her plans, she takes a job at the eatery in the village, and ends up staying for the summer.

Abby's Dad – Bernard

Jackie – Abby's friend from England, who was already in Greece and had arranged the job Abby never made it to on one of the islands.

Rockie – Abby's dog

Sonia – Abby's new stepmum.

Mr Rodgers – Abby's physics teacher.

Uncle Brian – Has a model train set in the attic.

Stella – Runs the eatery in the village.

Stavros – Stella's husband.

Mama + Baba – Stella's parents. Stella's mama is a gypsy.

Aaman – A Pakistani illegal immigrant.

Alex & Liz – Run a cupcake shop in Saros.

Demosthenes – A bully who abused Stella at school but who is now older and wiser, and leaves generous tips when he eats at her eatery.

Juliet – An English woman who lives in the village and gives Stella English lessons.

Mick – Juliet's husband

Kyria Katerina – Lives opposite the church, was a nurse. Suffers from arthritis. Cares for Marina.

Marina – A woman who lives in the village and runs the corner shop

Mitsos – A farmer who lives in the village

Mr Kleftis – A lawyer. 'Kleftis' translates literally as 'thief'.

Nektarios – A bully.

Nikos – A taxi driver

Theo – Runs the kafenio in the village.

Vasso – Runs the kiosk in the village.

Thanasis – Vasso's son, now in Athens.

Yiannis – Owns the Malibu bar where Jackie is working, and where Abby was hoping to spend the summer.

Book Club Questions - The Gypsy's Dream

+ If Abby had been older do you think that witnessing her being beaten would have evoked the same reaction in Stella?

+ Why did Stella not enlist Mitsos's help, or confide in him?

+ Did Vasso know what was going on between Stavros and Stella? If so, why did she not do anything about it?

+ What role does Juliet play for Stella? Would Juliet have had as much impact if she had been Greek?

+ What did Abby want from Stella apart from a job?

+ What put Abby and Stella on a more equal footing?

+ What was Vasso's role between Stella and Abby?

+ Why do you think Savros married Stella, and do you think she was aware of this?

+ In what way did Abby's view of her father mirror Stella's view of Stavros?

+ If Stella and Abby's and Vasso's business does not succeed do you think this will alter Stella's or Abby's self worth. If not, why not?

The Art of Becoming Homeless

As I write the introductions to the books, it is becoming clear to me that I feel such immense passion about the core subject that anchors each of them.

These days we all spend a significant part of our lives working in conditions or situations that are not always in harmony with our wellbeing. Often this is unavoidable. My question in this book is - is it? What would we have to do to escape what we have been led to believe is the inevitable? And would we be willing to do what it takes to make such a break?

The Art of Becoming Homeless is about an English woman who has followed the rules for years, and who is now successful but unfulfilled, and a Greek man who is trying to follow the rules, but just cannot manage it, and has quit his job. They meet and their mutual dissatisfaction helps them to question each other, and in the process they each find a path that will take them each to a more satisfying way of living.

Along the way they spend time with Adonis, Dino's best friend, who they believe is committing a crime. This drives a wedge between the three, as they each have their own views on what is morally acceptable.

In the book Michelle is significantly older than Dino, and this leads to some interesting questions about the nature of their relationship. It's not uncommon for a man to be the elder in a relationship, but it is unusual the other way around, and I was interested in the tension this would generate.

This book is partly about our struggle to free ourselves from the cycles that we unconsciously create, and about how it is easy to adjust to a higher income, but hard to let go of it once you have it - hence we call it a trap!

Cast of Characters – The Art of Becoming Homeless

Michelle – The protagonist. An elegant woman who works as a lawyer, and who is completely unaware of how attractive she is. She lives in London and is dissatisfied with her job and with her relationship with her husband.

Juliet – Michelle's friend from school. Moved to Greece and bought an old farm house in the village.

Kyria Georgia – Juliet's neighbour in the village who loves to grow flowers in her garden.

Mrs Riley – Michelle's housekeeper. Her husband is Michelle's gardener.

Penny – Michelle's sister. They are not close.

Richard – Michelle's husband who is a manipulator and a charmer.

William – Michelle's colleague at the law firm in Bradford where she first worked in law.

Arnold Braithwaite – Head of Dulwater & Marown, the law firm in Bradford where Michelle worked.

Cyril Sugden – One of Michelle's clients when she was at Dulwater & Marown.

Sir Sloughlow QC – Michelle's boss at the law firm in London (Sloughlow & Grotchett)

Doreen – Secretary at Sloughlow & Grotchett who is very chatty with Michelle and tells her all the gossip.

Dino – A young man who grew up on Orino, but then moved to the village. He has completed a degree in England but is now dissatisfied with the idea of long working hours and the high cost of living.

Dino's Mama

Adonis – Dino's childhood friend. Tall, handsome, athletic and charming. But also fiercely defensive over his friend Dino.

Koula – Adonis's mother.

Kyria Zoe – Adonis' aunt. Runs the pension where Michelle and Dino stay on Orino Island.

Uncle Bobby – Kyria Zoe's brother in law.

Fanis – Dino's childhood friend. An architect.

Ilias – Dino's childhood friend on Orino, water taxi driver.

Ilias 2 – Dino's friend in the village, runs a wood merchants, married to Florentia.

Themis – Dino's father, or at least that is what he would like us to believe!

Zahari – Dino's childhood friend. 'Zahari' literally means 'sugar', and is a nickname derived from the fact that he is diabetic.

Constantinos – Fisherman who supplies Costas Voulgaris's taverna on Orino island.

Costas Voulgaris – Hotelier, taverna owner and philosopher on Orino.

Flessas – Goatherder on Orino who helps when Michelle gets stuck

Josh – Child on the boat who picks up a cigarette packet

Panos – Hairdresser on Orino Island.

Markos – Panos' boyfriend.

Yanni – Donkey man on Orino island.

Suzi – one of Yanni's donkeys.

Dolly – One of Yanni's donkeys.

Book Club Questions - The Art of Becoming Homeless

+ Do you think Michelle would have escaped her job without Dino acting as a catalyst?

+ Do you think she was trying to escape her husband or her job? Or just find herself?

+ Was there ever a point when Michelle could have recognised the trap she had fallen into and that she could have stopped the roller coaster and got off the ride?

+ What do you think Michelle learnt about herself that she liked most?

+ Do you think Dino saw Michelle as a love interest from the moment he saw her?

+ What are the obstacles in a relationship where the woman is older than the man?

+ Have you ever reached that point when you felt stuck in your job, and what did you do about it?

+ If Michelle's house is an analogy what do you think it is an analogy for?

+ Do you think compulsory National service is good for a) the man and b) the country?

+ In what ways did Michelle help with the emotional difficulties Dino was facing?

+ In what ways is Dino freed by the confessions his father makes about his parentage?

In the Shade of the Monkey Puzzle Tree

In the Shade of the Monkey Puzzle Tree is essentially a coming of age story, and it follows Theo, the son of the *kafenio* owner as he travels to Athens to make his fortune and escape from the oppressive atmosphere created by his overbearing father.

When I first lived in Greece I had no money, and I took a number of low paid jobs to survive. One of these was in the Hard Rock Café in Athens (actually an imitation – not the official Hard Rock Café), and here I witnessed much of what is described in the bar where Theo finds work, so although this is a story it is also autobiographical to a degree.

The bar where I worked was a seedy place with a thin veneer of glamour, and it looked almost respectable at night, when the lights were dimmed and you couldn't see too closely into the corners. The way the business was run was ugly, and the head barman had his fingers in the till, and young girls were exploited; paid very little and made to stand at the entrance to attract customers.

The experience was a real eye opener and I have not had to embellish it at all!

The flats where Theo lived while he was in Athens are based on places I have stayed. The first place, in what was basically the cellar rooms of a grand old house had a door next door to mine, and after living there for almost three months I discovered that the second room, still packed with the landlady's belongings, had a cot in it and this sleeping place was being rented to a Pakistani man. This old lady didn't actually kick me out in the way described in the book but when I gave in my notice there were many similarities to the story told here.

The flat with the balcony was another I rented and it really did have an Albanian couple living in the basement, and they were expected to tend the garden in return for a free place to stay. Next door there was a family of gypsies living in a tiny run down little building that probably should have been condemned.

Athens is a fascinating place with lots of interesting corners like this. It's a city of contrasts, and the arrangement that the Albanians had negotiated didn't seem as odd as it sounds. Neither did the fact that the gypsies lived next door really shock me. Although I don't like to see injustice, I love the variety that can be found in Athens, and the way in which it constantly surprises.

In the book, Theo finds his way back to the village of course, and he realises that what he was searching for in Athens was there inside him all along. At some point we all have to make that transition to independence, and then later we have to stand back and watch our children go off and become their own people.

I wonder how much my own decision to move to Greece had something to do with my own coming of age story. I was thirty when I went, I had no money and at that time no skills. I had been lost in the UK having not found my path so it seemed just as valid to be lost in Athens where at least the sun shone. The reality was it was an experience that taught me to be independent and self-reliant and in the end I was in Greece simply because I chose to be - not because I needed to be.

Cast of Characters – In the Shade of the Monkey Puzzle Tree

Theo – The protagonist. Son of the *kafenio* owner in the village, he has grown up helping his baba serve coffee and subsequently has taken orders from his father all his life. But he wants to be his own man and so he goes up to Athens to find his place in the world and make his mark.

Yanni – Theo's baba, who is an old man.

Dimitra – Theo's mama, loving , kind, maternal.

Anastasia (Tasia) – Girl in the kafenio in Athens. A fiery character, who knows her own mind.

Lambros – Tasia's Baba.

Andreas – Kiosk owner in Athens.

Riya – Gypsy who lives next door to Theo.

Gorgi – Gypsy living next door to Theo in Athens. Riya's brother.

Timotheos – Baker in Athens.

Eleni – Timotheos' wife.

Margarita – Timotheos and Eleni's friend, and Theo's second landlady in Athens.

Margarita's mother – lives in the block of flats where Theo stays.

Bob the dog – Margarita's mother's dog. Later Theo's dog and friend.

Marinos – Margarita's mother's gardener. Lives in the basement at the house that Theo rents.

Aikaterina – Marino's wife.

Markos – Marinos and Aikaterina's son.

Theo's first landlady in Athens (unnamed).

Dimitri – Manager at the Diamond Rock Café in Athens. A very shifty character.

Jimmy – Bar man at the Diamond Rock Café who has made an art out of skimming money from the till into his pocket.

Leonora – Girl employed by Dimitri at the Diamond Rock Café who wants to become a model.

Makis – Bouncer / DJ at the Diamond Rock Café.

Phaedon – Owns the building where the Diamond Rock Café is situated.

Aspasia – Girl in the village with no real grip on reality. The other villagers know her and look out for her.

Cosmo – The village postman.

Cosmo's Baba –A farmer in the village.

Iro & Panayiotis - Couple in the village.

Manolis – A villager. Bullied Theo at school.

Martha the widow – A woman from the village whose house is destroyed by earthquake.

Mitsos – A farmer in the village. Theo's old school friend.

Mr & Mrs Papadopoulos – Couple in the village.

Old Spiros – Ran the last taverna in the village, that closed some years ago.

Stella – Runs the eatery / *ouzeri* in the village.

Thanasis – Donkey breeder in the village.

Old Odysseus – Keeps chickens and grows aubergines on the outskirts of the village, above the riverbed, where mattresses and other debris are dumped.

Stathis – A farmer in the village.

Vasso (short for Vasiliki)– Runs the kiosk in the village.

Damianos – Theo's friend from school, now in America.

Book Club Questions - In the Shade of the Monkey Puzzle Tree

+ Why did Theo have to put the physical distance between him and his father for a while to be satisfied with working at the *kafenio*?

+ Was he wrong to take the money?

+ Was his father wrong not to pay him a wage?

+ Do you think he handled the old lady and the rental of his first apartment well? What would you have done differently?

+ Do you think he should have told the boss that the manger was stealing?

+ Do you think it was right that he took from the till so the manager was not found out when he moved to the smaller bar? If not what should he have done?

+ Do you think Theo was responsible for the manager's legs being broken?

+ Do you think he should have turned over the money to the boss, or was he right to give it to the family that lived under his flat so they could return home?

+ What would your answer have been to the question he asks Anatasia?

+ When Theo returned home his father was ill. All in all would you say that it is harder to be the parent or the child in the coming of age process?

A Handful of Pebbles

It sounds rather a miserable subject for such a lively book, but I wanted to explore what the term 'depression' means to different characters and if indeed depression really exists in the way we commonly understand the word.

So I looked at it from four different angles. Sarah, the protagonist, has an underlying sadness that has been with her since she lost her first love. Liz, her friend, uses alcohol to mask her dissatisfaction with her life. Nicolaos, the shepherd, shows how the choices we make can keep us in or release us from sad places, and finally his mother Frona refuses to believe in such a thing as depression. She allows herself to be human, to feel her sadness, neither encouraging it or fighting it.

Like all the books in The Greek Village Collection *A handful of Pebbles* is based on real events. I heard the story that inspired the book first hand from a young woman who had set out with a friend to 'bag' themselves rich husbands by spending beyond their means and joining an expensive golf club on the Isle of Man. When I met her they had both found themselves husbands, one a lawyer and one a pilot. The girl married to the lawyer was truly in love and he helped her amass her own wealth by building up a property portfolio. Her friend had not married for love and she found herself in the role of unpaid nurse to the ex-wife, who had a terminal disease.

Around the same time I met two other girls on the Isle of Man who had come over from Ireland. They were with one of their brothers and he had hired a mobile burger bar for the TT races. Their plan was to make enough money to go to London.

It was an unfortunate year for the TT Races as a rider died, and not even during a race, but afterwards when the road was still closed. The TT is a famous motorcycle race that takes place on the winding, narrow lanes on the Isle of Man. If you ride a bike you'll have heard of it. There's not much protection for the riders – most of the narrow roads they race along are flanked by stone walls ...

The stories merged in my head and A Handful of Pebbles was born.

There is plenty of reason for all of these people to either be delightfully happy; after all they had all got what they set out to get: spouses, money etc. But they also each had reasons to be miserable, as their prizes always seemed to come with additional clauses. It was intriguing to see which character chose what and why.

Frona, in her attitude, I would like to think is probably most like me!

Cast of Characters – A Handful of Pebbles

Sarah – The protagonist. An Irish woman who comes on holiday to the village, staying at Michelle's holiday let cottage. Whilst there she takes the time to reevaluate her relationship with her husband.

Laurence – Sarah's husband is 64 years old, 15 years older than Sarah. A pilot.

Finn – Sarah and Laurence's son. 28yrs old. He is opening his own company selling media space to business startups in return for shares.

Helena –Finn's fiancé. She was born in the village but her family moved to Australia when she was young, then America and she moved alone to London. She works as a freelance photographer.

Jim – Helena's father.

Rudolph – A friend of Jim's from Germany.

Maria – Rudolph's wife.

Frona – Helena's grandmother, Jim's mother.

Nicolaos – Greek Australian shepherd. Frona's son.

Nikos – Frona's brother

Nikiforos – Frona's husband, deceased.

Jenny - A teenager, related to Helena. She loves dogs.

Joss – Sarah and Laurence's son, Aged 29yrs. He works in Finance.

Pru – Joss's wife. her full name is Prudence but Sarah secretly calls her Pruella de Vil. She is 30, born in the US, lived in Hong Kong, London and Douglas and sells software. She is good at her job.

Liz – Sarah's friend from school. They moved from Ireland to the Isle of Man together but 30 years later Liz moved to London with her husband Neville. Two years later Neville's mother died. Liz had tended her for 24 years.

Neville – Liz's husband, 68yrs old, 17years older than Liz.

Torin – Liz's brother.

Bernard – A friend of Torin's on the Isle of Man.

Damianos – A man in the village

Juliet – An English woman who moved to Greece and bought an old farm house in the village.

Mick – Juliet's ex husband.

Marina – Runs the corner shop in the village.

Michelle – An English woman who moved to the village and bought a house which she now operates as a holiday let.

Mitsos – A farmer in the village.

Stella – Runs the eatery / ouzeri in the village.

Theo – The kafenio owner in the village

Jeremy – A lawyer in the Isle of Man

Book Club Questions - A Handful of Pebbles

+ Do you think Sarah and Liz's reason for going to the golf club and having lunch with Laurence and Nev was morally acceptable?

+ Do you think Laurence and Nev's reasons for dating and marrying Liz and Sarah were morally acceptable?

+ In what way did the Torin's death change the girls?

+ Do you think Sarah's view of Torin changed over the years? Was it realistic or romanticised?

+ Did the memory of Torin help or hinder Sarah over the years?

+ Do you think there was any truth in Frona's views on the psychotherapy profession?

+ What role do you think Pru served for Sarah?

+ How did Juliet help Sarah?

+ Was Nicolaos right to go back and try again with his wife when he clearly loved Sarah?

+ Was Sarah right to leave Laurence and stay in Greece?

The Unquiet Mind

Yianni the donkey man intrigued me since he first showed up in Black Butterflies. He was based on a real donkey man I met on Hydra Island nearly seventeen years ago, who lived high up on the top of the island and came down to the town every day. Around the same time I went walking high on the ridge and met a woman bottle-feeding a kid outside her tiny shepherd's hut.

I was not sure what the story was about Yianni. I just wanted to explore his character, but after writing his story and getting it edited, and on the point of publishing the book I discarded the whole thing. It wasn't right. A couple of months later I tried again but it still would not come.

It was when I was recalling a girl who came to me for therapy once, having witnessed someone stab themselves up through the underside of their chin so she could see the blade flash in the light inside their mouth that it came to me that what I wanted to look at was what made us content, and what made some people very discontent. Obviously this man that she witnessed stab himself was very discontent!

The donkey man on Hydra, on whom Yanni's character is based, seemed to be a content man but something told me that there was a thread that ran through him, a niggle of something deeper that was discontent.

Katerina, the nun who helps Yanni through his life, is very content - but is that because she is a nun, or is it just her character?

It was interesting to explore all the things that made Yanni content and discontent, working through his understanding of the world and the part he had to play in it.

The ending, as is often the case, wrote itself. Having worked as a therapist I know that true healing is often the result of the unconditional love one person can extend to another and that all people are loveable if you sit with them long enough and understand them deeply enough.

Cast of Characters – The Unquiet Mind

Yanni – The protagonist. Born on Orino and happily living high up on the ridge of the island. He is mostly content and likes his own company. He works as a donkey man hauling goods and people from the port to their destinations.

Babis – Yanni's cousin. A lawyer who lives in the village. He is full of drive and energy and tends to be single minded, and consequently often does things without regard for others.

Dolly – One of Yanni's donkeys.

Moro mou – Yanni's first lamb. Literally translated it means 'My baby'.

Suzi – One of Yanni's donkeys.

Yanni's baba

Yanni's mama

Sophia – Yanni's childhood sweetheart who left Orino island after a terrible event and was brought up by the nuns in a convent near the Greek village.

Angeliki – Sophia's sister.

Miltos – A taverna owner on Orino island. Angeliki's husband.

Sada – Sophia's sister.

Aleko – A fisherman on Orino island. Sada's husband.

Sotiria – Sophia's sister. Married an Athenian and now lives in the US.

Sophia's baba – A Fisherman on Orino island.

Vetta – Sophia's sister, who started a lace making business and did not marry.

Damianos and Old Maria – Two villagers who have decided to sell their houses because of reports that the properties in the village unsafe.

Gerasimos – A lawyer based in Saros. Babis' rival.

Juliet – A British woman who has bought a house in the village.

Mick – Juliet's ex husband.

Terrance – Juliet's son.

Thomas – Juliet's son.

Cheri – Thomas's fiancé.

Marina – Runs the corner shop in the village.

Mercedes – The new donkey that Yanni buys from Thanasis.

Mimis – One of the donkey men on Orino island.

Sarah – English woman who lives in the village and works as a shepherdess

Spiros – One of the thugs who abducts Yanni.

Stella – Runs the eatery /ouzeri in the village.

Mitsos – A farmer. Stella's husband.

Takis - One of the thugs who abducts Yanni.

Thanasis – Donkey breeder in the village.

Theo – Runs the kafeneio in the village.

Vasso – Runs the kiosk in the village.

Costas Voulgaris – Restaurateur and hotelier on Orino island.

Hectoras - A donkey man on Orino island. Sophia's suitor.

Bibby – Hectoras's mule.

Sister Katerina – A nun who lives in the monastery near to Yanni's house on Orino island.

Tolis - A donkey man on Orino island

Book Club Questions - The Unquiet Mind

+ Do you think Yanni was only motivated to go the mainland to buy a donkey. If so do you think he went of his own free will or did sister Katerina manipulate him?

+ Do you think Babbis was aware of what he was doing to Yanni?

+ Do you think the real reason Yanni kept accepting drinks was to be social? If it was something else, what was it?

+ In what way could Yanni have made it easier for himself to see Sister Sophia?

+ Do you think Yanni was right to go home without finding Sophia?

+ Were Sophia's parents right to send her to a convent?

+ What would be the outcome these days if a suitor treated a thirteen year old the way Hectoras treated Sophia? Would it make a difference where in the world they were?

+ Do you think that there was a positive side to the years Sophia spent in the convent?

+ What did Juliet represent for Sophia?

+ What happened after Sophia answered the knock on the convent door on Orino Island when she was tending the garden for Sister Katerina in the penultimate chapter?

Watching the Wind Blow

A member of my family operates a charter yacht in the Greek islands. One day he awoke to the sound of the engine running and, sleepy-eyed, went up on deck and was met by the barrel of a gun. A pirate had taken charge of his boat.

The order of events in the book are more or less as they happened.

I have used this story as a backdrop to explore the concept of the Stockholm Syndrome. The Stockholm Syndrome, or capture-bonding, is a psychological phenomenon first described in 1973, in which hostages express empathy and sympathy and have positive feelings toward their captors, sometimes to the point of defending and identifying with them.

What happens in the mind of someone under the stress of being held against their will, especially when they are just a random choice, when there is nothing personal in the event for them? Does their true nature come through, do they assess their lives, do they put up barriers? We are all different and I am sure that we would all behave and think in a different way but there must be something that we all have in common for the Stockholm Syndrome to have become a recognised response.

In my younger years, when I lived in Athens there were times when I had very little money and life felt unstable. I met people who had witnessed and experienced things that they would rather have had no part in. Gathering a group of the most memorable stories, I presented them all as Irini's history and I allowed her to explore them during her ordeal on the boat.

Cast of Characters – Watching the Wind Blow

Irini / Rini– Lives in the village, and cleans Captain Yorgos's boat in Saros town.

Angelos – Irini's son.

Bun bun – Angelos's cuddly toy (a rabbit).

Dierk – Irini's mother's brother in law.

Glykeria – Irini's cousin.

Petta – Irini's husband.

Marina – Petta's mother. Owns the corner shop in the village.

Costas – Minds the shop for Marina.

Stathoula – Irini's cousin; Glykeria's sister.

Yiayia – Irini's grandmother.

Sam – A mercenary who takes over Captain Yorgos's yacht. His real name is Peter.

Babis – A local lawyer.

Captain Yorgos – Operates a charter yacht out of Saros harbour.

Artemis – Captain Yorgos's yacht.

Demosthenes – Port Police Commander in Saros town.

Stella – Runs the eatery in the village.

Theo – Runs the kafeneio in the village.

Tolis – *koulouri* seller. A *koulouri* is a bread ring with sesame seeds eaten all over Greece for breakfast.

Book Club Questions - Watching the Wind Blow

+ Was Irini brave?

+ Did she do the right thing in contacting the port police?

+ What made her soften towards Sam?

+ Did Sam show any signs that her feelings were reciprocated?

+ What was it in the situation that brought Irini's memories to the surface?

+ When she was evicted from her family home what other choices did Irini have?

+ What do you think Irini's Grandmother was suffering from?

+ If you had such a grandmother how would it affect your view of the world?

+ Was there anything that Irini could have done to save Sam?

+ Was it 'dirty' money? Should she have handed it in/given it to a charity?

The Reluctant Baker

As a teenager I witnessed some of the events that are related in The Reluctant Baker. One particular teacher went into his stock cupboard with two of the girls at my school on more than one occasion. The same teacher married one of his pupils soon after she left school. Somehow it all felt normal; people around me treated it as normal but to me it felt shocking and I couldn't understand why no one else felt about it as I did.

When I did bring this subject up with my mother she talked a lot about duty and obligation and other concepts that made no sense to me in this situation and the more I questioned the more the implication was that I was too young to understand.

So, aged 53, I thought maybe I was now old enough, and so I decided to explore these ideas of obligation and emotional fidelity and stretch them as far as I could, to see where the breaking point was for the two characters involved.

It was purely by chance, or the co-ordination of the universe, or however you like to view these things, that the witch hunt against celebrity paedophiles started in England around the same time that the book was release, with Jimmy Saville being one of the first to be found guilty of taking advantage of his position.

Cast of Characters – The Reluctant Baker

Ellie – The daughter of an English vicar and his wife. He preached to her heavily on morality, to the point of making Ellie feel unloved and uncomfortable in her own body. So when a teacher showed interest she was curious, and responded to the attention. However, they were caught in a compromising situation which was made public. The result was the press hounded her and made her persecuted and isolated. She never actually planned her trip to Greece, reality having become so distorted with the press following her.

Becky – Ellie's school friend. A bully.

Ellie's parents

Marcus – Ellie's husband and pottery teacher. He delights in being free and experimenting and experiencing in life - no matter who it hurts.

Brian – Marcus's boyfriend. Works as a history teacher at the same school.

Penny – Ellie's school friend. A bully.

Loukas – The village baker who met a girl from the village at university and married her for all the wrong reasons. She died six months later and Loukas was left holding her parents' family business together. He is unhappy.

Loukas' father in law

Natasha – Loukas' wife, deceased.

Stheno – Loukas's mother in law who is used to getting her own way. She is sly and sneaky, both of which she believes are ways of being clever.

Babis – A lawyer in Saros town.

Iason – A farmer in the village.

Fillipos – Iason's son, who likes to go running in the mornings and dislikes nightlife, drinking and smoking.

King Nev & Queen Helen – A couple who live in Little Lotherton.

Kyria Poppy – Shop owner in the village.

Sarah – Receptionist at Stella's hotel.

Stella – Hotel owner in the Greek Village.

Mitsos – Stella's husband.

Theo – Café owner in the Greek village.

Vlassis – Assistant deputy planning officer in the town hall in Saros.

Book Club Questions - The Reluctant Baker

+ Was Ellie right to take a break from Marcus? Should she have let him know what she was doing? Would it have made a difference?

+ In what why do you think Ellie's father role in the community affected the way he and his wife treated the situation with Marcus and Ellie?

+ What options do you think where open to Ellie other than marrying Marcus?

+ Do you think Ellie's expectations of a two week holiday were unrealistic?

+ Do you think Loukas should have stayed on at the bakery after his first wife's death?

+ Grief can come and go in waves. Do you think Loukas's first wife's parents were feigning their tiredness to some degree? If they were is that justifiable in any situation?

+ Would it have been wrong for Loukas to have pulled them up about it?

+ Do you think Stella should have told Loukas that Ellie was married? Or was she right to leave them to sort it out by themselves?

+ Was Ellie's only option to return to England when the situation became to intense with Loukas? What else could she have done?

+ Do you think Marcus should have been prosecuted? If so for what?

+ Do you think the experiences Loukas and Ellie have from previous relationships will draw them closer together, or do you think they might have damaged their trust in their fellow man?

The English Lesson

I wrote The English Lesson to explore the implications of a relationship that is characterised by a pattern of long term psychological abuse.

In this kind of a relationship one of the partners undermines the other in small ways and over time this behavior leads to all sorts of pain and suffering for the other partner, but without any obvious outward signs such as the bruises.

Often the psychologically abused party is not completely aware of all they are suffering, which is subtle, and tends to create to a general lack of confidence. This can be difficult to recognise for what it is, especially from within the relationship.

What I wanted to look at with this book, was a relationship of this type, where the effects of subtle long term bullying had created a situation for the bullied partner where almost any alternative was preferable; where the partner was so undermined that her very existence felt under threat. To an outsider Toula and Apostolis's relationship would not have appeared remarkable, whereas in fact Toula felt profoundly lonely and increasingly isolated by Apostolis's selfish attitudes, to the point where we are given to believe that she was prepared to leave him in a lift stuck between two floors when she went off to visit her relatives in another country.

If this is what she did was she in any way justified? Did his systematic bullying over the years justify her actions towards him? Did she have any other options if she wanted to get out of this toxic relationship? Could she, given the circumstances and the social pressure that she would have faced, have just stood up to him and announced that she wanted to end the relationship? Would he have listened if she had asked him to change? Would Toula even have been capable of articulating what the problem was, and how he made her feel?

I wanted to explore the moral issues faced and experienced by someone in Toula's position (and it is perhaps worth noting that it is not always the woman who is the abused in a relationship) and ask whether there is any justification for the way she behaved. I also wondered how the law would view Toula? As I mentioned before, she had no bruises to show, but the damage done to her over the years was perhaps more serious that a black eye.

In this novella I do not make it clear whether sweet little Toula has a hand in her husband's death or not, and I prefer to leave that for the reader to decide. From the emails I have received it seems that opinions are split fairly evenly, which of course highlights how it is our own frame of reference that determines what we see, or what we think we see.

Cast of Characters – The English Lesson

Toula – An elderly woman who moved to Saros from the village with her husband Apostolis. Their relationship was good when they first married, but he has withdrawn from her over the years and she feels isolated.

Adonis – A young man who lives on Orino Island. Dino's friend.

Alyssia – Toula's daughter

Apostolis – Toula's husband, who doesn't pay her much attention.

Dino – A young man who lives on Orino Island. Michelle's boyfriend.

Emilianos – Waiter in a café in Saros.

George – Apostolis's business partner in Athens.

Juliet – An English woman who lives in the village. She gives Toula English lessons.

Katerina – Toula's granddaughter – 3 years old.

Michelle – Juliet's friend who has bought the house next door in the village Michelle is the protagonist of The Art of Becoming Homeless.

Terrance – Juliet's son.

Thomas – Juliet's son.

Yianni – A taxi driver in the village.

Zephyria – A woman who lives in the village. A friend of Toula's.

Book Club Questions – The English Lesson

+ In what way do you think taking lessons from Juliet affected Toula's decision to visit her family in England?

+ Does Michelle play any part in Toula's decision making?

+ Do you think that Toula picking bougainvillaea symbolises anything for her?

+ In what way did Apostolis bully Toula?

+ Is there any way Toula could have dealt with Apostolis's bullying if she had addressed it earlier in their lives?

+ Why do you think Apostolis did not fix the lift?

+ Why do you think the electricians did not respond to Toula asking them to come and fix the lift?

+ What was the significance of the cat to Toula?

+ Do you think Toula was responsible for her husband's death?

+ Do you think there was any justice in his death?

The Priest's Well

I enjoyed writing this book so much! I wanted to write something a bit darker but without resorting to blood and guts, murders and so on.

Savas, the protagonist, was based on a priest I came across online who had risen and fallen in the church hierarchy a couple of times and it seemed that no one could decide where his motives lay. He seemed to be doing the right things, but in the wrong way.... So this was the question I set myself. What happens if someone we traditionally define as being good, in this case a priest, is actually not, and vice versa. How difficult is it for us to reframe our thinking?

I set out to have the priest as the rough diamond hero and the girl as the oddball with the intention of switching the roles through the story to see how easily I could redefine them and accept the new definition.

I didn't know how the book would end when I started writing, and I will be honest - Nefeli surprised me in the last few pages!

Cast of Characters – The Priest's Well

Savvas – The new priest. The protagonist.

Savvas' Mama

Nefeli – Savvas's housekeeper

Nefeli's Mama

Aleko – Runs a garage in the village

Babis – A lawyer in Saros

Bishop - ***Introduces Savvas to the village.***

Cosmo – ***The village postman.***

Kyria Maria – A woman in the village who lives opposite the church. A busybody.

Marina – Runs the corner shop in the village.

Mitsos – A farmer in the village.

Sotos – Savvas' predecessor.

Stella – Runs the eatery / ouzeri in the village, and the hotel on the beach.

Book Club Questions – The Priest's Well

+ Why do you think the church moved Savvas from one country to another and was it the right thing to do?

+ Should Savvas have been put so far out in the countryside or do you think they should have kept a closer eye on him?

+ What do you think his predecessor's true motive was for giving Nefeli the bigger house?

+ Do you think the fall down the well traumatised Nefeli, and if so in what way?

+ One of the seven deadly sins is gluttony. What does the opening scene of this novella tell us about Savvas's character?

+ Do you think the finding of the diary advanced the situation between Nefeli and Savvas? What should he have done with the book?

+ Do you think Nefeli was aware of what she was doing? Do you think she was plotting and scheming? Is there any evidence for that?

+ Do you think Nefeli moved back to the big house to gain control over the well? If so why do you think she never tried to tell anyone about it or gain access to it before the house was hers?

+ Did you expect Nefeli to leave the village? Do you think she will settle, what do you think she will do?

+ Did Savvas go mad? If he went mad is he responsible for his actions. When does the one end and the other starts, bad to mad?

A Song Amongst the Orange Trees

A Song Amongst the Orange Trees is a gentle story that explores both what it means to be a friend as well what we need in our lives to give it value.

Sakis's character, the protagonist in the book, is based on a friend of mine; let's call him John. John has struggled to become his own man as his larger than life father has always overshadowed everything he has done, if not in reality then certainly inside his head and heart. Having had such a strong character as a constant backdrop John almost didn't notice when a very gentle person befriended him. A friend who quietly helped him to become all he could be, a friend who brought out his softer side and then supported him as he found his integrity and his own identity.

It is very interesting that during the writing of this book a mutual friend of ours came to stay with me for a holiday. During this time, whilst I was struggling to find lyrics to the protagonist's pivotal song, this mutual friend, out of the blue, gave me a present of a poem he wrote, inspired by his stay in my home. In my mind it was a perfect fit for the lyrics of the song in the book and it seemed very apt that the words had been provided by a friend rather than me writing them - a true reflection of the nature of the book.

Cast of Characters – A Song Amongst the Orange Trees

Sakis – The protagonist. A singer / songwriter who represents Greece in a song competition and wins, but with a song that he considers musically poor. Following his success at the competition he must decide whether to retain his integrity as a musician, or follow the money and fame.

Andreas – Sakis' manager, who is much more motivated by wealth and fame than Sakis.

Costas – Sakis' Baba, known as Costas the crocodile killer

Antigone – A friend of Sakis' Baba who lives in Piraeus.

Antonis – Antigone's husband, a friend of Sakis' Baba who was considered to be a *Manga.*

Sakis' Mama – Died in an accident when her car reversed into the sea.

Sakis' Yiayia – Sakis' grandmother is mentioned throughout the book, but she died before the story starts, and does not appear as a character

Abby – An English girl, introduced to Sakis by Stella

Anna – A woman in the village

Bobby – A gypsy boy in Saros town

Eleftheria – One of Sakis' cats. Named after a well known Greek singer, Eleftheria Arvanitaki

Ellie – Receptionist at the hotel in the village

Grigoris Taxydaktylos – A clarinetist from Thessaloniki. Taxydaktylos literally translates as 'Fast Fingers'

Harris – One of Sakis' cats. Named after a well known Greek singer, Haris Alexiou

Jules – A journalist who sees life much more clearly than Sakis, but instead of using words he uses action to gentle guide his friend to happiness.

Katerina – A woman in the village

Stella – Owner of the hotel in the village

Thanasi – The donkey breeder in the village

Dora – Thanasis' sister

Yorgos – A villager

Book Club Questions – A Song Amongst the Orange Trees

+ Sakis grew up with the *mangas* (the 'hard guys') in Piraeus. So what influenced his approached to music and how might this be at odds with the song contest?

+ What was his motivation to go to America and how do you think this would have affected his work as a musician?

+ Sakis's success at the song contest had the potential to make him a lot of money, but he didn't feel that the song had any merit or integrity. It felt cheap. Which would you choose, money or integrity?

+ How important do you think it was to him to be invited to perform at the Greek village celebrations, compared the winning the contest?

+ How would you characterise the relationship between Sakis and Jules?

+ How would things have been different if Sakis had not contracted laryngitis?

+ Do you think Jules loved Sakis, and if so in what way?

+ Do you think Sakis was right not to go to America?

+ Do you think Jules was right to go?

+ What sort of relationship do you think Sakis may have with Ellie?

The Stolen Book

A British friend of mine who lives in Greece wanted her sons , who were born and raised in the village, to go to university in England for the education, but also so they could learn more about their heritage. Her father was in the British Army, and she was born when he was stationed in the Gold Coast – then a British colony. Then, the Gold Coast was considered to be a part of Britain, but is now the independent nation of Ghana.

To her surprise, when her boys applied to universities in the UK, they were told that they would be treated as foreign students, because the place where she was born is no longer considered to be British. Nor could her sons hold British passports, even though their mother has one.

She did not give up, and did everything she could (that was legal and honourable, I might add!) to get her sons to university and this is her story.

The added intrigue of someone stealing from the water board is another true tale that happened on one of the islands and I thought it was too good a story not to be included somewhere, so I amalgamated the two.

But underneath this simple story of a woman's battle to do her best for her sons there is a question that arises: How much of what we do for our children is really for ourselves, and if we asked them if they wanted what we are offering, are we positive that they would agree?

Characters like Karolos, the protagonist's husband, appear a few times in the Greek Village Series: characters who are calm and cool and want little from life. I suspect they are there because they intrigue me. I find it very difficult to allow things to unfold naturally, and am always pushing for control, or more, or better and I have a secret suspicion that by writing about these contented people I am hoping a little will rub off on me!

Cast of Characters – The Stolen Book

Niki – Protagonist. Originally from Albania where her parents remained until they died. Niki now lives with her family in the village. She and her husband have always struggled for money and Niki's aspirations for her children exceed their means.

Karolos – Niki's husband, an orange farmer. A gentle man who accepts life just the way it is. He is grateful for all he has and seldom asks for more.

Grigoris – Karolos' brother, a farmer.

Petros – Niki's son

Spiros – Niki's son

Agnes – Maid in the hotel in the UK

Brian – Taxi driver in the UK

Frank – Con man on the bus in the UK

George the Greek – Café owner in the UK

George the Greek's cousin – Slum landlord in the UK

Zoe – Girl in the estate agency office in the UK

Constantinos – Manages the water board office where Niki gets a job.

Cosmo – Village postman

Irini – Marina's daughter in law

Juliet – An English woman living in the village, who gives English lessons.

Katerina – Girl who works in the water board office

Costas – Katerina's husband

Kyria Georgia – A woman in the village. Juliet's neighbour

Kyria Toula – Lives inSaros town. Niki cleans her house.

Kyrios Apostolis – Kyria Toula's husband.

Marina – Runs the corner shop in the village.

Mrs Appleton – Administrator at the university in the UK

Stefi – Woman behind the counter in George the Greek's café

Stella – Runs the eatery / ouzeri in the village, and the hotel on the beach.

Mitsos – Stella's husband

Stavros – Stella's first husband

Tasso – Orange buyer who owes Karolos and Niki money.

Themis – Rich kid, friend of Spiros and Petros

Vasso – Runs the kiosk in the village

Yianni – Village taxi driver

Yorgos – An accountant

Book Club Questions – The Stolen Book

+ Why do you think Karolos did not question Nikki's plans?

+ Do you thing Nikki was being realistic, or do you think she was naive to go the UK without firm plans in place?

+ What do you think were the greatest cultural differences between the village and the town in the UK?

+ Which of the boys do you think is most likely to stay in village and become an orange farmer and which, if either, do you think will become independent in the wider world?

+ Do you think Nikki was wrong to take the book from Toula's house?

+ What do you think Nikki's presence in the house meant to Toula?

+ How would you characterise Toula's relationship with her husband?

+ What do you think of Karolos's attitude towards the children? Why do you think he and Nikki had different attitudes?

+ How much does Nikki's past influence her parenting skills?

+ If the boys were to study at a foreign university might it make it difficult for them to return to the village in later life? From this point of view is it possible that Nikki was doing them a disservice?

The Rush Cutter's Legacy

In a taverna one night whilst I was island hopping, I watched a slight woman working away in the kitchen, and when the rest of the family took a break she was expected to continue her chores. I watched what I thought was an outsider to the family, a casual employee as she put down her tea towel and greeted a small boy who was brought into the taverna by the head waiter. The older stout bossy women who I presumed was the tavern owner seemed to bristle as this child called the slight woman Mama, and then turned to address the waiter as Baba. I watched the exchanges some more, and it became clear that the owner was the head waiter's mother.

I realised that what I had presumed initially was wrong, and that the dynamics in this family were far from cordial.

I stayed a day or two more and it seemed that the family's dynamics were far from private; in fact the whole island knew, and the plot for The Rush Cutter's Legacy was born.

As with all the books some of the more detailed events that are related happened to me, and I have woven them into the story, and some have happened to friends of mine so many of the details are realistic.

Cast of Characters – The Rush Cutter's Legacy

Vasso – The protagonist. A woman in her fifties was born in the village and having lived there all her life. She runs the kiosk and having been born in the village and her Mama before her she knows everyone who comes to buy things form her and usually they are related in some distance way. In her own way she has been very successful, but her life was not always like that. When she was a child she and her mama struggled for money and she started working at an early age.

Thanasis – Vasso's son.

Vasso's Mama

Spiros – Vasso's boyfriend, and later husband. He is a driven man, driven to make something of his life but even more driven to provide for those her loves.

Argyro – Spiros's stepmother. Runs the taverna on Orino island. Altogether not a very nice woman. She has become bitter thinking that the way he dowry was lost was unfair.

Augustinos – Argyro's father. Owned a kafeneio on the harbour front on Orino island.

Dimitri – Spiro's friend.

Stamatis – Spiro's father. Runs the taverna on Orino island. A kindly old man, but in the past he has been too kind and this comes back to cause him problems.

Anna – Stamatis' wife, deceased.

Theodoris – Spiros' grandfather

Christopher – A man on a yacht on Orino island.

Crystal – Christopher's wife.

Gabrielle – Christopher and Crystal's daughter.

Cosmo – A boy at Vasso's school. Now the village postman.

Juliet – An English woman living in the village.

Stella – A woman from the village. Runs the eatery across the road from Vasso's kiosk.

Gerasimos – Bank manager on Orino island.

Ilias – Fisherman on Orino island.

Kaloyannis brothers – Two brothers who manage the boatyard on Orino island.

Kyria Papadopoulos – A woman who lives on Orino island.

Panayiotis – Greengrocer on Orino island.

Papas – The priest on Orino island.

Stefanos – A donkey man on Orino island.

Leontia – An old woman who lives on the mainland. Spiros stayed with her and she taught him to cook.

Vasilis – Leontia's husband.

Book Club Questions – The Rush Cutter's Legacy

+ How much of Vasso's initial attraction to Spiros may have been induced by the excitement of the adventure that she felt she was having? Did she really love him or did she just need to be near someone who showed her love and comfort? What role does proximity play in romantic relationships?

+ Spiros's focus on his work created tensions in his relationship with Vasso, and caused her feel neglected. Was his behaviour unreasonable, and were her expectations unrealistic?

+ Their wedding was a very public affair. How would such a celebration feel to you if you were the center of attention? Would you feel joyful or stressed?

+ Do you think tight knit communities such as the one on the island can suffocate you, or do they create a feeling of belonging?

+ Agyro is presented as selfish and unkind in the tale but was she really? How much of her behaviour was excusable because of her life experiences?

+ Spiros grew up with Argyo as an overbearing and jealous step mother. How might this have affected his character?

+ What do you think about the way the village treated Leontia?

+ Was Vasso wrong to take her child and leave the island?

+ Vasso's husband died and then her son moved away to Athens with his grandfather - how must this have felt?

+ At the beginning of the book Juliet points out that Vasso never talks about herself. So why is she opening up now?

The Short Stories

The Eastern Fly

Grigoris sits under his olive trees, looking out over the plain where he grew up. Below him his village is spread out, a patchwork of terracotta roofs amongst the rows and rows of trees that surround the only place he has ever lived. And there, just by his cottage, are pinpricks of gold, the last oranges left in the expanse of green before him.

Grigoris is putting off going home to Lena. He does not know a kinder woman, and normally they never argue about anything, but this is the one area of disharmony between them. She's going to be furious, and he'll never hear the end of it!

Every year Lena tells him not to play this game with the oranges. His baba never played the game and Grigoris is not sure where he first got the idea, but for years it has worked well, so why should he not have played the game this year? It's so simple. All he has to do is wait. That's the game. Just wait. Then wait some more, until after Christmas, if possible, when everyone else in the village has sold their oranges. Then, when Sergei or Timur come to buy more, he can ask any price he likes, within reason. It's a simple game, but there is a catch. The fruit must be sold before February, when the frosts might come. One night of severe frost and the whole year's crop can be gone, and his income with it.

Today is the twenty-ninth of January and there is no sign of Sergei or Timur.

Grigoris sits with his back against the olive tree, holding his crook upright between his knees. He rolls the shaft in his hands and watches the hole its blunt end digs in the dust.

This game of waiting has worked for him for years and years. Every time, he has been lucky, and the prices he has commanded when everyone else has sold their oranges have made the old boys in the *kafenio* gasp and shake their heads.

'One year you're going to come unstuck,' Theo the *kafenio* owner would observe softly.

It looks like this will be the year.

The Russians have simply not shown up, and they are not answering his calls.

They were here in November and December, but since then no one has seen them.

He'll not hear the end of it from Lena.

A *vromousa* lands on his shirt. He is about to flick it off, but how many times has he been caught out like that with these bugs? Squash them, harm them, and they stink and you scramble to get away. The flickering olive leaves are shading him from the sun and his backside has moulded to the ground, and he feels very reluctant to move. So, instead, he picks up a fallen leaf and offers it up to the green bug, which carefully and ponderously crawls on board. He examines the insect for a moment, then puts the leaf with the bug down on the ground.

If the Russians don't show up in the next week, if they don't get the oranges picked soon, it will be the frost that takes the crop. The weather forecast on the radio said it would be minus three next week. It's hard to imagine that today, sitting in the shade of the olive tree to keep cool, but February is a deceiver, and a sunny day can be followed by a bitter frost at night. Lena will not understand. She will say, 'Turn on the fans, Grigori. Isn't that what they are for? Just turn them on and keep the oranges from freezing.'

But he can't turn them on. He hasn't told her, but the electricity has been cut off. He cannot pay the bill until he has sold the oranges.

She will nag him endlessly, not just now, but for years and years to come, dragging the subject up whenever she needs to score a point.

He looks down at his house. She is there, coming out of the back door, a basket under one arm to hang out the washing. For an old lady she moves well. Come to that, for an old lady she is still quite a looker.

He squints but from this distance he cannot make out her face.

If only he could think up an excuse, one she would believe.

He cannot say that no one is buying, because everyone else has sold, and he cannot say the oranges have not ripened, because they *have* all ripened. It has been a good crop for everyone this year. Maybe that is why Sergei and Timur have not come back. Maybe they have bought all they need already? But he cannot say that. The *vromousa* spreads its wings and flies vertically, landing on his shirt again.

'Flies! Yes, that's it!' he tells the bug. 'I can tell her that the oranges have some sort of fly, or weevil, and that until the pests are dealt with no one will buy.' And if Sergei and Timur never turn up he can say that the flies killed the crop. Will she believe that? She must have heard everything about oranges that there is to hear, either from him or from her baba before him. So this will have to be a new fly, a new bug, from the East. Yes, from the East, that sounds good.

She has left her basket on the ground, still half full of washing, but she is nowhere to be seen.

Perhaps he should go and tell her now, whilst it feels fresh and real.

Using his crook, he levers himself up from the ground, shakes the stiffness from his legs and begins the slow saunter down the hill. He will stop in the *kafenio* for a nip of ouzo to help him sound calm.

'*Yeia sou*, Grigori.' Theo wipes his table with a grubby-looking cloth. 'Coffee?'

'Er, no, an ouzo.'

Theo hesitates, but only for a second.

Grigoris could count the number of times he has had ouzo during the day on one hand, and Theo knows this.

'A nip of ouzo, or a fortifying glass?' Theo asks, no edge, very gentle.

'Fortifying,' Grigoris replies. Theo goes behind his counter and returns with a glass of clear liquid and a bowl of ice. Grigoris spoons in a single ice cube and watches the ouzo slowly turn cloudy.

'There will be no frost tonight, Grigori, nor tomorrow, they say.' Theo is fishing, but Grigoris ignores him and rehearses his lines inside his head.

'Hello, dear. Heck of a day. Still can't get rid of that fly …' 'What fly?' she will ask, and then he can tell her all she needs to know. Yes, it will work.

'It's a new fly from the East.' He spits this last line out loud, and a new, even more cunning thought occurs – if he starts the rumour here it will back up what he tells Lena later, or she may even hear about it from another source, and that will make the story so much more plausible.

'Fly? What fly?' It is Mitsos on the next table, who sold his oranges early – in November, if Grigoris remembers correctly.

'Oh, nothing that will affect you this year, my friend. Only my oranges, as they are all that is left.'

Mitsos turns to his neighbour, Cosmo the postman. 'Have you heard of this fly?' he asks, and Grigoris stifles a grin. If the postman knows about it, the whole village will have heard the news by morning. There may be no need to tell his wife a thing. In fact, he can say he was trying to keep it from her, to stop her worrying, but yes, sadly, it is true, they must pull their belts in, and it will be a lean year.

Brilliant! Grigoris is in high spirits now, and he throws a generous handful of coins on the table and makes his way home with a lightness in his step.

'*Yeia sou*, Lena,' he calls from the gate. She is in the garden, hanging the last of the clothes. Despite the ouzo and his earlier resolve, the nervousness is returning now that he actually has to face her, but as it turns out he needn't have worried.

'Ah, Grigori. I've just had Sergei on the phone,' she says, coming round the corner with the empty clothes basket in one hand. 'He says he is coming with trucks and workers tomorrow. He will meet you in the *kafenio* at ten to agree the price.'

Grigoris exhales with such force at this news that he feels a knot of muscle across his shoulders unlock so quickly that his arms go quite limp.

'You all right?' She studies his face carefully.

'Oh, yes, yes, quite, yes. Yes, Sergei.' He spots another chance to make himself look like he is in control. 'Yes, I wonder why he is calling again,' he bluffs. 'We had already decided tomorrow at ten. Maybe he's very keen this year, and the price will be higher than ever?'

Lena narrows her eyes at this, and Grigoris swallows, and fiddles with the keys in his pocket.

He sleeps so soundly that night that Lena has to wake him the next morning.

'You've overslept,' she gently chides him. 'By the time you have grazed the goats you will be late for Sergei.'

The goats are happy to be out, and the day is sunny with a clear blue sky, and particularly warm for the time of year. The animals are a little reluctant to return early but, once back in their pen, they drink thirstily from their trough. He should go to the *kafenio* now, to meet Sergei. Or maybe he should wait and be a little late, make it look like he is not keen. That might push the price even higher. Yes, he will make his way to the *kafenio*, but he will not hurry.

The sun is beating down from a cloudless sky again, and Grigoris is aware of the sounds of the village around him. Birds sing and call to one another, hidden up in the trees and bushes on either side of the road. A dog barks in the distance, and a tractor rumbles somewhere behind him. Up on a slight rise ahead, smoke curls gently upward, marking a bonfire where some farmer is burning the prunings from his olive trees. Away in the distance, the sea sparkles, and

Grigoris has to narrow his eyes against the glare. The sun's heat on his limbs has a gentle, soothing effect, and the day seems full of possibilities, as though the whole world is waiting for him. Grigoris is aware that this feeling is helped along by his anticipation of a healthy profit, and he calculates figures in his head. The bills will all be paid, of course – that would be the sensible thing to do, and he will be able to announce to Lena that they are no longer in debt to anyone. A new tractor would be nice. Not exactly a new one, of course, but a slightly newer one than the rusty old Zetor. And then, maybe, there will be a little something left over to treat themselves. Perhaps a holiday? Yes, that would be the thing. Not to anywhere too fancy, but maybe to Orino Island, which they say is a romantic destination. A holiday, and a little time to focus on one another again, like they did when they were courting. Lena is still a good-looking woman, but neither of them is getting any younger. These thoughts bring Grigoris to the steps of the *kafenio*, and he is reluctant to walk up them out of the sunshine. But Sergei will be waiting, and the negotiations must be conducted.

'Ah, Grigori,' Theo welcomes him. 'Coffee?'

Nodding, Grigoris looks around for Sergei. Mitsos is there, but not Cosmo, and Babis the lawyer has cornered poor old Socrates and is talking fast, leaving no opportunity for Socrates to reply. But there is no Sergei. Choosing a table by the window so as to spot him when he arrives, Grigoris waits for his coffee. Theo never hurries; he expects to wait.

'Here you are.' Theo puts a cup down on the table.

'What time is it?' Grigoris asks.

'Eleven thirty.'

'Eleven thirty?' Has he missed them? Is it possible that his plan to look as if he isn't interested has backfired?

'Yes, why?'

'Oh, I was supposed to meet someone.'

'Oh, yes, Sergei. He rang,' Theo says.

Grigoris's raised eyebrows lower again, a smile breaks over his lips and his breathing becomes more even.

'Yes, they said not to worry about them, they can go to the next valley, where apparently there are still some oranges.' Theo takes the tea towel from over his shoulder and wipes his hands.

'They have gone elsewhere?' Grigoris asks incredulously. 'Why?'

Theo frowns.

'They said that they eat the oranges from the inside out, so they look fine but inside there is nothing.'

'What do?' His heartbeat is in his ears.

Theo frowns in return.

'The Eastern Fly, Grigori. The Eastern Fly.'

The Letter

The square stone building stands three storeys high, just across from the harbour. It is topped with lovely old terracotta roof tiles, and the ground floor was long ago turned into a taverna and sold off separately from the upper part.

In the summer sun the stonework is a honey colour, the shutters a pale blue-grey. Just beyond the building, the heat shimmers off the tarmacked road that runs parallel to the sea. The building's position affords spectacular views across the bay.

Nikki holds the big key in her hand. It's her key now. It slides and then settles with a satisfactory clunk as she puts it in the lock of the high, ornately carved wooden double doors. They creak as they open, as they have always done. This problem, if indeed she decides to consider it a problem, is now hers. Just as she is entering the house, a cat she recognises as Toula's appears from the shade of a bougainvillea bush across the street. It seems strange that Toula would leave the animal behind. It's not as if Toula ever really wanted a cat, but in the time Nikki worked for her the animal seemed to make a real point of befriending the old lady. It was Toula's husband, Apostolis, who refused to let it stay.

So the cat lives out on the street, where it always did, and begs for scraps of fish from the tourists at the tavernas. In any case, Toula divides her time between the village and London, where her daughter and grandchildren are, and the house in Corfu, and she could hardly be expected to take the animal with her. It's a friendly little thing, and it ingratiates itself by rubbing its chin around Nikki's ankles, but as soon as the door is open wide enough it shoots inside and up the stairs. Nikki follows it in.

With a cursory glance at the lift, as if she almost expects to see something there other than polished wood and ornate metalwork, she takes the stairs. Stairs she has washed and polished a hundred times, if not more!

At the top, the door is open, revealing the room beyond to be pleasantly bare. The tapestries that hung on the walls have gone, along with the heavy dark furniture. Most startling of all, but definitely the most satisfactory too, is that the ticking of Apostolis's clock collection is now absent. The place is empty and it looks a lot bigger than it did when it was full of Toula's and Apostolis's lifetime collection of furniture, memorabilia and junk!

Without hesitation, Nikki steps towards the nearer of the French windows, that lead out onto the balcony. There are two balconies at the front, one at the side, and one at the back. With energy and joy Nikki delights in swinging open first the tall windows and then the louvred shutters. Each balcony has an elaborate wrought-iron railing and cantilevered supports of carved stone. As she flings open each set of doors, the sun streams into the room, lighting the place up in a way she has never seen before.

It is hers, all hers!

Outside, over in the harbour, the halyards clatter against the masts of the yachts moored there. The occasional moped or car passes on the road below. The taverna in the lower rooms will be shut at this hour but there is still chattering, because two women have chanced to meet and are talking directly below one balcony at the front. Many years ago, Toula planted a fig tree in a pot on the side balcony ... and now it has grown so big the balcony is cracking under its weight. One of her first jobs will be to remove both tree and pot. If it is possible, she will plant it in her own garden, behind her house in the village. She steps onto the balcony gingerly, but it is still solid. Toula used it every few days to haul groceries up from the street, using an electric winch that Apostolis fitted there for his mama. The motor would whirr as it brought up vegetables or lowered the dry cleaning. It spared Toula's old legs the strain of the stairs. Toula, to Nikki's knowledge, never used the lift. She always said that it was unsafe, and now she has been proved right.

A brief frown crosses Nikki's brow but she consciously forces it away. She will not give any credibility to the rumours. She could not, will not, believe anything evil of Toula, who was a kind, dear old woman. How could someone give a gift of their house with one hand and murder their husband with the other? Could such a divided heart exist?

Nikki sighs. No, she does not believe it, and in any case she is not sad about Apostolis. He was not kind and she never cared for him. He barely acknowledged her. In all the time she worked for Toula, cleaning and keeping her company, she cannot recall even one time that Apostolis actually spoke to her, not directly.

'Tell her not to move the clocks,' she can remember him saying once. Why had he not asked her himself? Was she too lowly to be spoken to?

'I don't want these windows open.' That was on one of her first visits. 'The sun will fade the colour on the woodwork.' He was referring to the longcase clock he was winding at the time. But even though he and Nikki were in the same room, the comment was addressed to Toula who, head wobbling slightly from side to side, left the vegetables she was slowly chopping in the little annex off the big room, which they had turned into a kitchen, and pottered over to where Nikki was polishing the legs of one of the over-padded sofas.

'Would you mind, dear,' she said softly, 'not opening the windows? My husband thinks the sun may fade the antique woodwork.'

With all the windows open, Nikki turns to survey what is now her kingdom, hands on hips. She cannot help but smile. Despite the age-buckled floor, it is a beautiful room, with really nice proportions.

But what's that? The room was completely empty when she came in, she is sure of it. Yet, now, there in the middle of the floor is a sheet of paper. With a quick glance at the windows she wonders if it could have been blown in. It's possible.

It is thick paper with uncut edges, and it is covered with neat handwriting. A shopping list? No, it is more like a letter. Curiosity triumphs, and Nikki scans the first line.

He is not kind. As his mother it feels traitorous to say, but it is the truth. Apostolis is unkind.

The page has Nikki's full attention now. All thoughts of where it has come from are swept aside. Trying to smooth the paper, helping it to uncurl, she reads on, stepping backward until her back is against the wall between the two front windows. She slides down the wall until she is seated to take the weight off her now-trembling legs. This is Apostolis's mama's writing: a voice from the grave. Nikki shivers.

He has never really been a kind boy, not even when he was a child. Determined, perhaps, but not kind. He did the usual macabre investigations into ants and spiders and how many legs they could live without, but I had to stop him when I caught him being unkind to puppies or kittens. My wish was that he would grow out of such behaviour, but he continued to be just as cold and unloving as a teenager. There were never any hugs for me. But I took hope because when he met Toula, he seemed to change. He smiled more, was attentive to her. They began their lives together and he managed to share with her in a way he had never shared anything before. He shared his space, and his possessions. As a mama I was so happy and I loved Toula so much for bringing out the best in him.

Then when he took the loan from the bank to do up Toula's old cottage in the village, I thought he was finally being kind. Making their home beautiful, maybe even putting in a nice new kitchen for Toula. Pretty young thing that she was back then … But I should have known better. He used the money to buy some rough land, and the cottage was forgotten as he went in with a shifty-looking builder from Evedaros. He built and sold two houses on that tiny plot of land he bought. It was all decorated entrance halls and bad foundations. There was no pride in the work. Poor Toula. But she stood by him, did his accounts and sweet-talked the buyers. She was marvellous for him, but he could not see it. He bought more land with the money from the sales and began to build again, and then he got in with that man from Athens, thick as thieves they were, him and – George, I think it was.

It is strange how things fade, the things that are less important. I suppose I do not need to make my peace with them so I do not remember them.

Well, when Apostolis started to work with whatshisname-from-Athens, the first thing the stupid boy did was to squeeze Toula out of the business. Stopped her doing the accounts, put the money into a bank account that she has no idea how to access. Then he wanted to get his hands on my home, the cottage in the village where I was born, where my mama was born, where Apostolis himself was born. Oh, the promises he made, the sweet talk he spent hours delivering until I was worn away.

No, really, I felt worn out with him. I just wanted it to stop, so I gave in. Well, he built a whole line of houses on the land attached to my old house and that was when we moved here, to this big old windy house that bakes in the sun in the summer and freezes in the sea breezes in the winter, and no sooner were we here than I could just feel that I was now a nuisance to him.

Sure, he put in a winch for me to haul up the weekly shop but it was like the houses he built – all show. His top lip curled when I spoke to him. He took his meals in his study rather than sit with me and Toula.

You see, unlike Toula, who was so kind, I would draw his attention to anything questionable that he was getting up to. It was my duty. I am his mama. But he did not like it, not one little bit.

I will not go into the various details of all the unkind and dismissive things he did to me, but Toula would squeeze my hand to let me know she was there to support me. Bless her. And now they are saying such unkind things about her. If only they knew.

So one day I faced him. I told him the way he treated me was unacceptable. He sneered and went to wind one of his clocks. I grabbed his sleeve and he pulled his arm away with such a jerk I nearly fell. I was eighty-eight and my strength and balance were poor. He did not put his hand out steady me.

'You think they would treat you any better in a home for the elderly?' he asked in a voice that made me think he was quite serious.

'You wouldn't?' I was terrified at the thought. I was finding living away from the village hard enough, but the idea of being shipped off to live with strangers …

'No, I wouldn't,' he said, and just for a moment I thought he was softening, maybe even recognising the care I had given him all his life. His back was towards me as he wound and wound his clock and, as he said no more, I contemplated his posture and the words he had just said and I realised that he would not send me to a home for the elderly because they cost money, and he was not about to put his hand in his pocket for me!

The next day was the first time strange things began to happen. The rug in my room, by my bed, had been carefully folded over so I nearly tripped. If I had fallen, my head could have hit the rock I use as a doorstop. I would have been a goner. Rugs get rucked up all the time, you could say, but two days later there were dried chickpeas out on the balcony when I went to haul up the vegetables. My foot skidded, they were like marbles. If it had not been for Toula coming out just at that moment my head would have hit the wrought-iron railing and that would have been that.

But he has always been a determined boy and so naturally he did succeed. It was in the lift a week later. I had been down in the lift the day before and I knew it was working just fine, so the following day I naturally stepped into it to take the rubbish down and out. The lift seemed to be descending a little faster than normal, I thought. The speed increased and I was just about to cry out when the whole think jerked to a sudden stop not far from the ground. The jerk was so sudden that I swear I felt my brain hit the top of my skull and as my neck snapped back I saw, just for the most fleeting of seconds, a clock-winding key jammed in one of the cogs that worked the lift. Even in so brief a moment, I could see that it was done so that the cage would jam just above the ground with a shock that rattled all my bones, bounced my brain and snapped at my neck. But it was my heart that gave way. It beat furiously, thumping through my chest and then, as if someone had tied an elastic band around it, it struggled but could beat no more.

I saw myself slump to the floor, my face ashen, my left hand twitching, alone. But even if anyone had come at the time, there would have been nothing that they could have done.

Half an hour later Apostolis came out of the door at the top of the stairs. He usually took his precious lift but this time he trotted down the stairs, calm as you like, leaned over the roof of the stuck carriage, retrieved his clock-winding key and went back upstairs, leaving Toula to come in from having coffee with friends to discover the lift jammed and me lifeless from a heart attack on the floor.

It shocked Toula deeply. Her face went white, her head began to shake on her neck and from then on she developed this little wobbling movement she does when she is nervous. Well, I would be nervous too if I had to live with Apostolis after that.

The doctor said it was natural causes. I think that is what they always say when someone as old as I was has a heart attack. Toula cried and cried, and then she put the advert in the downstairs window for a cleaner. I don't think she could stand the thought of being alone with him.

Well, I could have left but there was unfinished business, you see. As far as I was concerned that was murder, what my son did to me. So I bided my time. I watched over Toula to make sure she was safe. I discovered that I could go into animals' bodies if I wanted to go outside, and there was this beautiful black cat who didn't seem to mind a bit. It was nice when Toula stroked me, like we were connecting again, and I did my best to give all my love back to her through her hands when she did touch me.

The other thing, apart from enjoying being in a cat's body, was that I found I could stop things. Mechanical things. Like his clocks. I would stop them just to annoy him and he would spend hours tinkering with them but to no avail. I practised on those clocks, stopping them, grinding those little wheels to a halt by the power of my will. I would stop two of them at a time so he would get exasperated, running from one to the other. But it was all part of a greater plan.

Finally, I saw a chance. Toula was going to England to see their grandchildren, my great-grandchildren. Brave girl, she had broken free of Apostolis a little by then. She made it clear that if he did not want to go then she would go alone, and she arranged it all. Once she was in the taxi to go to the train station, I became impatient. They were meant to be going together in that taxi but Apostolis was finding excuses to make them late. So in the end Toula went on her own. But from the moment she was gone I was not going to waste any time.

Apostolis, my son, my murderer, stepped into that lift, and I did the easiest thing in the world. I stopped the cogs, right between floors, so he was stuck.

At first he began to tinker with the buttons and the concertina cage doors, but whatever he fixed I unfixed. The lift juddered up and then down, but only by a fraction.

When he began to call for help it did pull at my motherly heartstrings, but he had tormented me as boy and man and had shown me no love. He was just as cold to Toula, and their children had also suffered. Their grandchildren, thank goodness, had never met him.

So there he was, stuck in the lift, and there he was for two weeks, in the summer's heat, with no food or water, and he was not a young man. He did call, and shouted out, at first. But the walls and acoustics of he old building didn't carry the sound. He remained undisturbed until poor Toula returned from seeing her grandchildren. But she has an instinct, does Toula. Always had an instinct, and she called on the electrician to go with her to fix the lift on the day of her return, so it was he who found my son with no life left in his body.

So I guess that sets the record straight – there should be no more gossip about Toula now! I have made my peace.

There is a sudden and loud bang from one of the upstairs rooms, and Nikki jumps and shivers at the same time. The sun is still streaming in through all the windows but the cold is noticeable. The noise in the room above repeats itself. She stands slowly, leaving the paper on the floor, then ventures to the bottom of the stairs.

'Hello!' Nikki calls up. Unlike the main room, the staircase and hallway are still gloomy. The noise came from Toula and Apostolis's bedroom.

'Hello.' It is also dark at the top of the stairs. There is no window on the landing. She switches on the light and it all looks familiar again. But as she nears Toula's bedroom door she sees it is slightly open. It is not pitch dark, but with both shutters and curtains closed the room is in gloom.

As she pushes the door and flicks on the light, the black cat, its pupils dilated, jumps from the bed, flashes past Nikki's rooted feet and streaks soundlessly down the stairs and out of sight before she can blink.

On the floor, a bedside lamp rocks on its side. The mundanity of the fallen lamp, which must be what caused the noise, comes as such a relief that Nikki laughs at herself, a dry, humourless sound.

After switching off the light and shutting the door firmly, she returns downstairs. She will take the paper home and see what Karolos, her husband, makes of it. Probably someone's idea of a joke. It is in very poor taste.

The sun fills the room. She will find furniture that is modern and light and fresh to complement this space.

Nikki scans the floor for the letter, but it has gone. She left it just there on the floor, but it is not there now. There is no breeze, no draught, nowhere it could be hidden. The paper, the account of Apostolis's death, has disappeared.

She leaves shortly afterwards, almost doubting her senses, and never does see that sheet of paper again.

The next couple of weeks are spent decorating and furnishing the flat. Nikki will rent it out to tourists in the summer, but for now today her work is done.

As she closes the door, it occurs to her that since that day, since the day of the letter, she has not seen Toula's cat again either.

ΤΑΒΕΡ

A Pair of Blue Eyes

Easing herself out of her chair, Poppy makes her way slowly to the front of the shop. Racks of clothes crowd her on either side, threatening to engulf the narrow corridor that is left down the middle of the shop. Poppy has collected far more than she has sold over the years, and the result is that the tiny shop is filled to overflowing with her eclectic collection. The glare on the window highlights the grime, but long ago she became selective over the use of her energy, so the dirt remains and her days pass in subdued tones. But if she does not lower the blinds before midday the shop will become stifling hot, more than she can bear.

She steadies herself as she goes, a hand on an old-fashioned diver's suit complete with brass helmet, then on a rack of cheesecloth shirts. She stops to use her toe to push to one side a roller skate that has made an escape from its partner, then continues her well-worn path to the open door and out into the sunshine. There is not much trade to be had on this little backstreet in the village, but it supplements her pension.

Poppy's grip is not what it used to be and each day it seems to take longer to turn the handle that lowers the tarpaulin shade. But she is in no great hurry, and presently the awning is lowered, shading her window, and Poppy returns to the back of the shop to settle herself comfortably in her chair again. Her eyelids droop and she slips into a pleasant place halfway between dreams and memories.

Not far from her Athens home, a younger Poppy slows to a halt over the double yellow lines outside the kiosk, her front inside wheel mounting the kerb, her seat belt caught in the driver's door, on the kiosk side. It is like any of the thousands of kiosks all over of Greece, originally installed to provide employment for war-wounded soldiers. The wooden sentinel boxes are all the same size and a uniform mustard colour, and have become part of the landscape. Some have been expanded, with drink cabinets added, and extensions to the roofs – for shade, and to claim a little more of the pavement.

In this particular kiosk the magazines and newspapers, which would no doubt once have been pegged on rope around the booth, now stand in a purpose-built magazine rack.

Poppy gathers a handful of the local papers. 'I ordered a magazine on interior design in the name of P. Metavolis?'

It never seems to be the same kiosk attendant twice these days. Long gone are the wounded soldiers; it is all family businesses now, and families seem to have a never-ending supply of cousins.

It is winter and Athens is grey in the early morning half-light, the unlit shopfronts reflected on the wet pavements, traffic hissing by slowly, lights on. It has just stopped raining. Adjusting her focus, Poppy smooths her hair in her reflection. It's a practical style but too short to tie back. Behind her, high on a hill, towers the Parthenon, majestic and solid, magnificent even in the damp weather.

Weary to the bone, Poppy manages a smile for the shopkeeper, who looks blank and yawns, flashing gold somewhere in the recess of his nicotine-stained mouth. Poppy deposits the papers on the counter and rummages around in her bag for change. She sighs as she finds she used all her small notes at the wholesale warehouse. The man behind the counter rolls his eyes as he takes her large-denomination drachma note.

Coat flapping, she squeezes back behind the wheel and throws the magazine and papers onto the passenger seat. A lone box of *kolokithia,* missed earlier, occupies most of the back seat. She will take it in later. The girls have enough fresh produce for now.

She pulls the dangling seat belt across her lap as she switches on the lights and points the car homeward. Argon will still be asleep, sprawled across their double bed, mouth slack, reeking of alcohol. Yesterday she thought that finally the day had come. He presented her with a ring box: old, antique-looking. She waited for him to drop to one knee, to announce his love. To say something like, 'After fifteen years of being with you I could not be surer that we are destined to grow old together.' But he didn't. He waited for her to open it, her stomach in knots, floating, sinking, turning. The anticipation must have shown on her face – her wide-eyed joy. But he did not really even look her in the face.

Instead, he flatly said, 'Found that. You might want to let the customers know, see if anyone dropped it.'

Poppy's stomach growls with hunger and she scans the street for a parking space by the cafe on the corner. A secret moment to herself reading her magazine, a *bougatsa* and a sweet coffee that she does not have to make herself will keep her going.

As she approaches, she is disappointed to see that the cafe is closed. She must be earlier than usual. But a place just a little further on is open – or at least the lights are on. The wheel hits the kerb again and, after she slips out of the car, the seat belt resists Poppy's attempt to close the door. The establishments seem to change hands so quickly these days. She hopes it is a cafe with a corner where she can read her magazine.

The shop's interior looks bright and cheerful, but it is hard to tell if they are serving yet or just setting up. Inside, a man in a high-waisted long white apron, working behind a counter, helps her overcome her hesitation by beckoning her to enter. He is only just visible between the words *So* and *Sushi,* which are written in an arc on the window.

'Sushi,' Poppy says to herself. Is that Japanese or Chinese food? Either way, she has never tried it.

The door to the establishment is freshly painted, and a young man is on his knees fiddling with it, fitting a new lock. He has dark hair that contrasts with his bright blue eyes, and Poppy tries not to stare. She has heard such colouring is a throwback to how the Greeks were in ancient times. The man smiles and doffs his peaked cap, releasing his curls, and steps to one side to let her pass. It is an action performed with humour, and Poppy feels a long-forgotten thrill of attraction at the eye contact he makes. The wooden floor springs underfoot, as if she has lost ten pounds in a heartbeat.

After examining the sushi menu and deciding what she wants, Poppy sinks gratefully into a comfortable chair in the corner, with a plate of food, a cup of coffee and her magazine. The back of the magazine is uppermost, displaying an advert for dog food. A picture of a schnauzer dog stares, blue-eyed, back at her. Poppy lovingly strokes the picture for several seconds before turning the periodical over to open the glossy front page, the insides spilling over with ideas for her business and her home. She feels quite light-hearted as she settles down to enjoy the next twenty minutes.

Reading about free-standing baths, Poppy awkwardly manipulates the chopsticks that came with her plate of Asian cuisine as she dips a roll of sushi into the small portion of green paste. 'Wasabi paste,' the man behind the counter called it. There isn't much of it, and she would never serve such a mean portion in her taverna. Scooping half of it up in one go – to really try the food properly, as her mother would have said – she readies herself to anticipate the flavour. Fifteen years of running a fast-food outlet with Argon and serving *souvlaki* has made her a picky eater. The meat for the kebabs in her shop rotates all day long in front of a grill, slowly cooking from the inside out, and slivers of meat are shaved off with a long, sharp knife throughout the day, wrapped in pitta bread with chips, tomatoes and tzatziki, and served to appreciative customers. At first, the meat was whatever the butchers supplied, but over the years she became fussy, went to oversee what was put in it, insisted on finer cuts of meat. This attention to detail, Poppy feels sure, led to the success that allowed them to open a taverna, which she has been running for two years now. They are full every night. So busy that, in the last fifteen years of living together, in an Orthodox country, no less, Argon has repeatedly convinced her that they do not have the time to get married.

Poppy turns to an article with ideas for underfloor lighting and pops the sushi roll with the green paste into her mouth.

A wasabi firework explodes into the back of her nose, spreading like an electrified acid stream up her sinuses. Her eyes promptly try to dilute the sensation with a flood of saline, her hand catapults to her nose and she holds her breath, wondering if the feeling is going to subside or cause permanent damage.

She loves it!

The interior design magazine slides to the floor as Poppy picks up the sushi menu. Her nerves return to normal and her eyes temper their generous flow but the menu does not give her the information she needs. 'Sushi', 'wasabi paste' ... Perhaps if she returns home quickly she can take fifteen minutes to look it up, find a reference in one of her many cookery books, before starting on the accounts.

Another sigh escapes her. The accounts will take hours and she needs to do them before Argon is up and about, demanding coffee and clean underwear. She wonders if he will bother to go in to the taverna today. As usual, she has no idea what time he came home last night.

Selecting a family-sized takeaway box and three tubes of wasabi paste, Poppy pays the bill. Her magazine lies where it fell under the table, the abandoned dog's doe eyes uppermost.

The lock-fitter smiles as he holds the door open for her again and Poppy feels a surge of chaos inside as her excited response to him, her loyalty to Argon, and her new-found passion for sushi all battle for centre stage. The tag on his overalls declares he is Nektarios from *Kleidi* Services. He clears his throat and puts his cap back on. Poppy smiles and heads for her car. The early morning grey is giving way to bright sun and the tarmac steams slightly as the damp evaporates.

The car door doesn't shut properly before Poppy sets off, but the forward motion of the car clicks it closed and she drives one-handed, pulling at her seat belt with her other hand, only to reverse the process moments later at the house.

Muttering to herself, she mentally organises her day as she marches up the path. Every day she takes a couple of hours to meet with planners, builders and officials at the new shop, a second taverna. Keeping this new venture a secret from Argon has not been difficult. He seems to have lost all interest in any aspect of the business, no matter what she does to try to engage him. His only real delight is the money in his pocket at the night's end and whom he can impress with it.

She enjoyed taking this burden of work from him in the early days, when the two of them ran the *giro* shop. Now, managing the accounts by herself is just how it is, like changing the sheets, or going to the produce market before dawn.

The second taverna is going to be the climax of all her long-term passions – her passion for business, her passion for interior design, her passion for food. She hopes it will thrill Argon. This second restaurant is going to be a surprise present for his fortieth birthday.

She can picture him already, appearing late in the evening, just before closing time, fluttering from table to table. Building social networks, he calls it, gold cufflinks on a shiny white shirt, open-necked, showing his jade pendant on his hairy, tanned chest. Just as he does now in the first taverna. It is a bittersweet image if she thinks about it for too long. It is wonderful to see him feeling so successful, but on the other hand his habit of coming in late results in him always inviting the remaining diners to go on to a bouzouki club with him. In this department, Argon is a generous man, free with both money and time. Poppy is always asleep by the time he comes in; her days start as his finish. They never seem to celebrate their success together.

She closes the front door and drops her keys onto a patch of pollen under the flowers on the hall table. She takes the time to pop Kyria Katharo's money under the vase ready for her weekly visit, lest she forget later.

Poppy pauses to look into the mirror behind the flowers. She smooths her hair and licks her lips, sliding them together, finally pouting, trying to ignore the wrinkles, before dismissing her reflection with a dissatisfied sniff. These are not the years for vanity; this is a time for work. There will be a season for preening somewhere in the future.

Before turning to the kitchen, she looks up to the ceiling and lifts her chin, testing the air, ascertaining by the stillness that Argon is not yet up.

With the family box of sushi in the fridge, she flicks the kettle on and lugs her tired weight across the sitting room. Her aging skirt stretches to its limits as she walks, causing it to ride up. The sun streams in the window, highlighting motes of dust that spin and swirl in the gently moving air.

There is evidence of Argon's late-night return: the TV guide on one of the sofas, a coffee cup balanced on the over-padded, oversized chaise longue, a styrofoam box from a half-eaten takeaway from the restaurant on the red lacquer coffee table, and a fork on the floor. The rest of the room spreads large, designed, and unlived in. The room is an expression of their wealth, their separation, her loneliness. Poppy exhales and fights a wave of unexplored, denied feelings. She holds tight to the feeling of blankness that has become her norm.

She picks up the fork from the floor and tosses it on the coffee table as she crosses the room to a door disguised as a bookcase: the door to the study. It is her place of work after the produce market and before the taverna.

The study is small and cosy, with a desk and high-backed swivel chair, and a floor-to-ceiling bookcase. Poppy studies the titles and selects *Gourmet Food from Around the World,* and finds the entry for sushi. Her mind instantly feels light, absorbed in a new interest, free again.

She is about to turn the page when she accidentally kicks a pile of car magazines that Argon has been clearing out. The top one slides to the floor and some papers fall out – small squares of paper, notes. No doubt Argon has been making note of makes, engine sizes and all the other incomprehensible details to do with cars that give him such a thrill. Curiosity prompts her to pick one up. It is a square of lined paper, torn from an exercise book, and on it is written *Argon? Can we talk?* in swirling, rounded, girlish letters.

Poppy's stomach turns backward, her temples abruptly seem to be compressing her skull, her eyes glaze with tears and her lungs are held in suspended animation. She waits for the sensations to dissipate, as she did after the wasabi paste shock. But the perturbation deepens, nausea settles into a heavy weight in her chest, and all her self-doubt, gathered over the last few years, passes through prisms of fear and resolves into what she has known all along. She deflates into the chair.

The rush in her ears is the sound of all her unborn dreams imploding and the shards slicing through her future, her safety, her ego, her stability, her love. All that she thought she has, and is working towards, spins into her peripheral vision and vanishes, leaving a chasm of pain spiralling back towards her.

Steeling herself, she fills her lungs to get oxygen to her brain, grips the edge of the desk and focuses her vision. 'It only says "Argon? Can we talk?"' Poppy reminds herself as she picks up a handful of the other notes and drops them on the desk. A new wave of pain penetrates under her ribs as the scraps of paper, note after note, flutter and settle. She reads one after another. Nothing specifically intimate is mentioned, but there is a sense of familiarity in the way they are written. *Coffee? … The film was good … 1.30?* She skim-reads the lot and grows frostily calm.

Pausing to assess her feelings, words such as 'hollow' and 'lonely' come to her, but, above everything, she feels stupid. The truth is, she has known for some time, but she ignored the signs and now she feels foolish. How many of her friends and family know and haven't had the heart to tell her – or, worse, feel sorry for her?

Poppy flings open the windows and the shutters, and the sun blazes in. It is a sharp contrast to how she feels, but she wants the light, the clarity.

She has always approached their relationship in the knowledge that his needs are different from hers; somehow, her part of the deal was to make his life as easy as possible and, if she did this, she conned herself, he would naturally be doing the same for her. Fantasy!

The reality is that, even from the beginning, right back when he couldn't get the lease to start the takeaway in joint names, he began to retreat from her. Looking back, she can see it.

How else can she explain to herself their not getting married?

Oh, he had his reasons, and each one felt legitimate at the time. They were either too busy, or they needed to focus on the business because they did not have enough customers, or they didn't have the money for the kind of wedding he thought she deserved. But, even as they prospered, he still always wanted a grander wedding than they could afford. At the time she had thought these details so romantic, so passionate. She, however, would have just married him on the spot with no fuss necessary.

Gathering up the notes, she puts them back between the pages of *Sports Car Today* and replaces the magazine on the pile and exhales.

Back in the kitchen, she opens the fridge door and pulls out the family-size pack of sushi and, grabbing a tube of wasabi paste, she leans against the fridge, her feelings sweeping over her undiluted, eventually drawing quiet sobs from her, until, consumed, she slides to the floor, where all she can do is refocus on the sushi box in her hand. She sniffs her last sob away and opens the box.

Eyes streaming from the punishment and the pleasure of the wasabi paste, she eats until she cannot face another grain of rice, and allows everything to settle. With food numbing her feelings it is easier to accept what she already knows – that she lost Argon years ago – and so begin the assessment of what will actually change in her life now she is alone.

From a business perspective, there is nothing to lose: he is never there anyway. From an emotional point of view, she realises, with a certain sense of pity for herself, nothing will really change either. All she thought she had was just in her head.

'No, absolutely not! I am not going to fall into feeling sorry for myself.' Poppy blocks out a black hole that threatens to engulf her. 'Self-pity will get you nothing,' she tells herself. 'And …' – she draws the words out as a new thought comes to her – 'I want everything!'

Poppy lets this thought roll around in her mind and then seep around the weight of emotional pain in her chest until it ignites her passion. She becomes lighter, and yelps as the drive takes hold.

'Oh, yes, the lot. I'm going to have the lot! And Argon – ha! He can have exactly what he has put into our lives – nothing!' She rolls off the chair and her taut skirt tears up the back seam. She hates the skirt anyway. Tearing it off like an ungracious stripper, she whoops and skips her way to the bedroom, bottom wobbling in her overwashed, sagging, grey knickers.

She is brought to a sudden halt at the bedroom door. Oh my God, she has forgotten – he is still there, asleep. In her mind he was already history. He is prone, black satin sheet pulled over his head. Her elation melts into the white wall-to-wall carpeting. The shape of him is so familiar.

Poppy gasps, emotions flooding her in response to his outline, before pulling herself back. 'No,' she admonishes herself. Turning her eyes away from his form and opening the wardrobe, she chooses the dress Argon hates most, coincidentally her favourite, which she doesn't often wear, along with high-heeled boots that accent her ankles, the only slender part of her these days. She is going to shake herself up, quietly, gently.

The taverna opens for lunch with no sign of Argon. Poppy has known Alethea for over twenty years, since Alethea's girls – one now in the kitchen, the other two doing a wonderful job of waitressing – were all babies. The four of them make a great team and in truth have not needed Argon's supposed management skills for years.

Poppy dumps the box of courgettes on the counter, next to Alethea, who is polishing cutlery. Alethea smiles and looks up, but on seeing Poppy her smile flattens and her brow creases in concern, and it is only a matter of minutes before the whole story is related and Alethea is holding Poppy, soothing her.

The stream of tears is eventually broken as Poppy finds her strength again.

Poppy stammers through her tears, 'Alethea, how do you fancy being manager here, but now getting paid for it?' She does not wait for Alethea's response. 'We don't need him, right?' she asks, and with this the tears become hugs and even a little laughter before Alethea returns to the cutlery and Poppy, feeling more in control than she has done for years, goes back out into the sunshine.

Until this point her feelings have been unstable, but now, having taken some action, having claimed the taverna as hers, the question that begs to be answered is, 'What next?'

She turns at the corner of the street, where the bougainvillea climbs the wall and sheds a pink sea on the pavement. With her high heeled boots looking at odds with the translucent crimson leaves, Poppy has a revelation.

The weight in her chest lifts and her sinuses clear as the shackles of time-worn thinking break open.

The 'us' of her and Argon that she has always worked for was all a mirage. The takeaway and flat above were leased in her name, and she is the person who employs the man who manages it for them. Manages it for *her*, she corrects herself. The restaurant's lease is in her name, and the new shop, which Argon doesn't even know about yet, was bought in her name. To add to this, their home – *her* home, which she and Argon have lived in – she inherited from her mama.

She isn't even married.

'Oh my God,' Poppy exclaims to herself. 'My life is my own!' She allows herself to revel in the thought, for it to fill her senses, empower her stature, growing into a passion, not for Argon, not for the business, but for herself. She feels proud, she feels accomplished, she feels strong.

She lifts her chin, and is about to accompany this sense of potency with an appropriately liberating yelp, when she thinks of her home, and the feeling wavers. She pictures her home empty, with no Argon. She will rattle around in it, with no one to love. She is a woman of passion, and she needs to love someone, to dote on them, to work for them, to plan the future for them. Her energy comes from this passion.

'The passion of love. I need that,' Poppy whispers.

She will confront him. Argon will need to offer either a convincing explanation for the notes, or a strong renewal of his dedication to her. That or a clean break, no strings. It is up to him.

Sweeping into the house, she is vibrating with determination to make something happen.

He isn't there.

But his absence is not enough to curtail Poppy's determination to take charge of her life. Half an hour later, after a quick search in the telephone directory and a couple of phone calls, the doorbell rings.

'Good afternoon, Madam, how can I assist?' He has a hint of a village accent, a dazzling smile and the bluest of eyes. Poppy experiences the excitement of attraction all over again.

'Good afternoon.' She smiles shyly. 'Could you please change the locks, front and back?'

'Immediately,' the man promises, doffing his cap, his curly locks falling free. Nektarios grabs a screwdriver from his bag of tools, and before Poppy has returned with a cup of coffee he has the old lock out and a new one in place. A thrill passes through her.

At two o'clock the next morning, Poppy is woken by the sound of a key being tried in the lock. She stays calm, listening to the scratching at the door as the key fails to fit. Then comes a low muttering, an incantation of swear words floating through the keyhole, losing their power as they echo down the hall.

Poppy remains unmoved, curled up on the chaise longue.

'Poppy! Poppy, the bloody key won't work.'

She doesn't stir. She smiles.

'Poppy! Poppeeeeee ...'

But she is lost to him. She is a woman of passion. Feed her passion and she will grow and blossom. Stunt her passion and that passion has no choice but to find new pastures in which to ripen and grow. Poppy is lost to Argon's infertile world and now there is richer soil, another love, another passion.

They are curled up on the chaise longue together in mutual adoration. Poppy looks into his eyes and sees her love returned. She feels such a surge in her heart that she pulls herself closer. He nuzzles into her neck, breathing in her scent, drifting in and out of sleep. They fell instantly in love, in the time it took to have a cup of coffee. No history has been exchanged, no questions, no explanations, no small talk. Just deep, reciprocated, passionate love.

Poppy knows this passion is for life, as she pulls him closer and kisses him on the end of his wet schnauzer nose.

Poppy awakes from the memories that feel like dreams. No one has come into the shop all afternoon and now it must be near closing time.

'I did a good thing, selling the business to Alethea,' she tells the still air as she makes her way to the door. 'Let the young take over. Retreat from the bustle of Athens to this beautiful place.' She giggles a little to herself, happy to have reached the days that are past being competitive, industrious. She turns the key in the lock and then retreats to the stairs in the back corner that lead up to her own rooms. With a hand on the wall, she takes the stairs one at a time. She can hear him inside. She no longer has the passion she used to, she no longer needs it, but she does have love. As she opens the door to her flat, Argon greets her, now old and entirely grey.

'*Yeia sou,* Argon, my love,' she says. He is beside himself with his love for her and can hardly stay still. His whole body quivers. She puts a tender hand out to touch his face, stroke his ears. Argon, the son of her first schnauzer, responds by running round and round in circles.

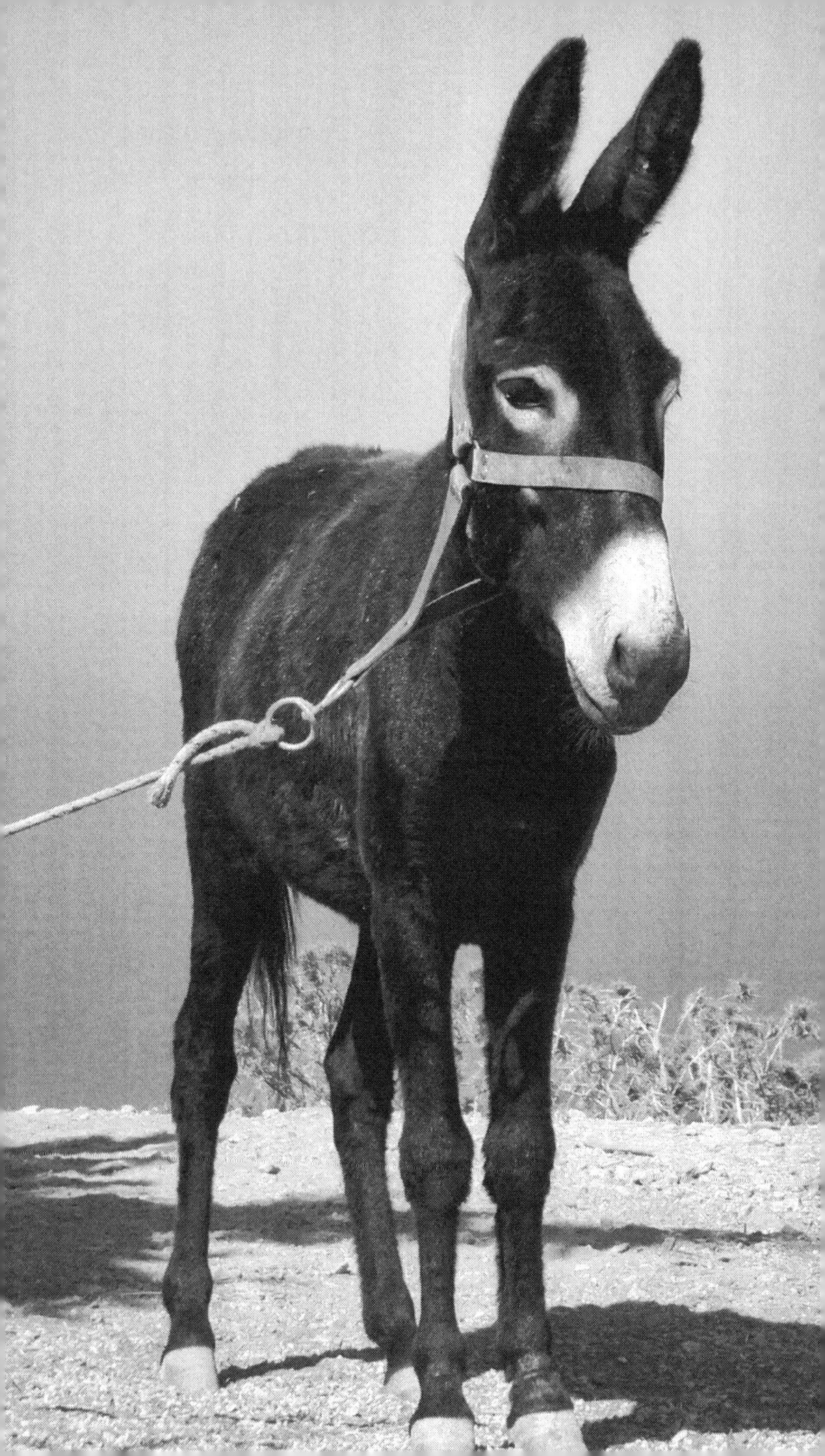

Mercedes and the Bird

Soft, blue-white clouds fill the sky, and even though the sun has not broken through all day the air is warm and the light gently bright. Everything is held in sharp contrast now it is nearly evening. The wisteria that hugs the wall of the whitewashed cottage has no leaves yet; it is a young plant and it is so early in the year. But last year's seedpods hang like pendulums. Most of the plants in their pots have yet to embrace the change in the season, except for the lemon tree peeking around the side of the house, which is not only in full leaf but abundant with yellow baubles.

The weather here at the top ridge means that plant growth always lags a little behind the rest of the island, but there is no hurry. The flowers are just for decoration. The plot Sophia tends for food is down within the monastery walls where the frost never bites and the heat lasts even after the sun has gone down. It is funny how everyone still calls it a monastery when for decades it has housed only nuns. Now it is home only to Sister Katerina. The last remaining nun is too old to tend her own garden, and so they have an arrangement that suits them both.

Sophia adjusts herself on the rush seat of her wooden chair. She is not so uncomfortable if she sits with her back straight, but some days the little mite is so full of energy that he, as Yanni says, or she, as she maintains, kicks and kicks until Sophia has to stand up and walk around to settle her. Soon it will be too much for her to tend the vegetable plot. But for the moment all is well, and right now she must concentrate on darning Yanni's socks.

She can see him, far away in the distance, down the hill. She spotted him and the animals as they emerged from the cover of the pine trees that grow along the top of the island. His hand is loosely leading Suzi, with Mercedes just behind, one animal leading the other, their long ears back slightly; they will be tired. As she darns, she watches him and the donkeys loom larger. He is carrying something over one shoulder. She darns and watches as he comes closer and closer.

'*Yeia sou*, my love.' He lets go of the donkeys' reins and they wander to the trough. '*Yeia sou, moro mou.*' He heaves off the heavy coil of rope that he is carrying and lets it fall to the floor, then bends from the waist and kisses her rounded stomach before going to the well to haul up water for the beasts. Their lips curl as they suck up the cool liquid.

'How was your day?' Sophia asks.

'Same.' Yanni stretches his hands above his head and closes his eyes. 'Mostly foodstuffs to the shops.' He refers to one of the many jobs the people of the island rely on the donkey men to do. With no cars or bikes, it is the donkeys that must haul the bottled water, the rice, the shampoo, the salt, the bedsheets, the roof tiles, furniture, everything everybody wants, from the cargo ship to the tiny shops dotted around the island's only town.

'Are you hungry?' She stands. She has cooked stuffed tomatoes, and they are ready in the kitchen.

'No.' The stretch seems to revive him and he continues with more energy in his voice, 'But I have rope.' And with this, he bounds around the back of the house and returns carrying a frame he has fashioned out of some fallen pine branches. He spent the winter hewing them, and with the addition of a few nails and some clever joints they now resemble a proper double bed frame. His excitement shows in his energetic movements. He ties the end of the rope to one corner and winds it over and back across the frame. With each turn, he puts a boot against the frame and pulls until the rope is taut. When it is done, he trots inside the house and returns with the thin single mattresses from the beds they have been using up till now.

'Ha ha!' Sophia laughs. 'So, we are to sleep out here, are we now?'

'Try it?' Yanni adjusts the mattresses so they lie next to each other and then stands with hands on hips to admire the completion of his winter project.

Leaving the darning on her chair, Sophia sits tentatively, as if she is expecting the whole thing to collapse. But it feels firm so she lifts her feet and lies back, fingers linked on her chest.

'The sky looks so big.' The clouds have cleared; now there is not even the trail of an aeroplane, just blue.

Yanni sits beside her, then lies down too, and they roll into one another, face to face.

'Well, this is going to be cosy.' Sophia laughs.

'Within a month or two that is going to keep us apart.' He puts his hand on her belly.

'Don't call her "that". They say they can hear everything, you know.'

Yanni wriggles and puts his head on her belly. 'Your mama is sorry she called you a "her" when you are a little boy.' He looks up at Sophia, his curled moustache twisting. He is teasing her.

'Say nice things to her, Yanni – don't tease.'

'I am to speak to your belly?'

'No, you are to speak to our child, just as you will when she is here.'

'When he is here I will tell him stories and we will play games.'

'Tell her a story now.' Sophia stops straining her neck to look at him and lies back again.

'You want a story, my little boy?' He smooths Sophia's dress over her belly. 'Shall I tell you one about two donkeys?' He looks over to his animals. They are standing now with their eyes closed, their working day done. 'This is a story about Mercedes, because she is a young donkey, just a baby like yourself. And just like you there is much she must learn about the world.

'So, when I first brought Mercedes up here she looked about her and she did not know where she was or what she was meant to do. So I let her off the rein and she and Suzi wandered over the hillside, eating all they could. But Mercedes wandered over to the edge of the pinewood there, and on a branch a bird was singing.'

Sophia lets out the briefest of sounds, almost a chuckle, but much more relaxed and content. Yanni seems encouraged by this, and he props his head on his elbow and continues with his narrative.

'"You sing so beautifully," Mercedes told the bird. "What are you?"

'"I am a bird," the bird replied.

'"Oh, I want to be a bird," said Mercedes, "can I be a bird?"

'"How can you be a bird? Birds sing," said the bird.

'Mercedes was much put out by this response, so she wandered off, over there.'

Yanni points west, along the island's ridge.

'Soon she came to the doors of the monastery, where the monks were about their evening prayers, chanting away. Mercedes listened and then said to herself, "I can do that." And so she let out her wobbling "heeee", but when she needed an in-breath she did not let this become a note, she sucked in the air silently, and when she had breath again, she let out another "heeeee". There! She was singing, and so she returned to the bird and proudly performed her one-note song.

'"Can I be a bird now?" she asked.

'"No," said the bird. "Birds have feathers."

'Again, Mercedes went away sad, and this time she wandered to the back of the house.' Yanni points east. 'There she found the chickens and she gathered up all the fallen feathers and she pushed them under her bridle and into the soft fur of her ears, and into the coarse fur of her legs, until she was covered all over with feathers. Then she returned to the bird.

'"I have feathers now, so now can I be a bird?" she asked.

'The bird looked at her from up on the branch, with a sideways look that birds give. '"No," said the bird again, "because birds can fly."

'Mercedes left, disheartened again, but as she neared Suzi, who was chewing away on the grass, she saw that hill.'

Yanni points south to a hillock above the house.

'So she climbed the hillock, and took a jump, hoping the feathers would make her fly. But she did not fly. She fell quite hard on her rump and all her feathers fell out. When she stood, she was very sore, but just then, Yanni' – he points to himself – 'came out of the house and took a scoop of meal and opened the barn door and called to Suzi and Mercedes. The two donkeys wandered into the straw-filled barn and began to eat, nose to nose, from the same bucket, and Mercedes said to herself, "Why would anyone want to be a bird when she can be a donkey, in this cosy barn, with a friend by her side and a master who loves her?" Then she closed her eyes and fell asleep.'

Yanni falls silent. Sophia doesn't move. Slowly, after some minutes of silence, he looks up to her.

'No, I'm not asleep,' she said, but quietly. 'But I'll tell you something, Yanni my man. You may not be the best carpenter in all the world, but you are going to be a wonderful baba.'

The Tractor

The men in the *kafenio* blink, sleepy-eyed, sipping at their first coffees of the day. Any talking is spasmodic: little snippets of news are exchanged with the least effort necessary. Later, the place will be noisy, with shouting and laughter, and the slamming of counters on the wooden *tavli* board, but the first coffee is a quiet one.

'My moped got stolen, from right outside my gate.'

Silence. The sun lights the tops of roofs as it peeks over the distant mountains, a line of shade across half the village. The floor-to-ceiling windows on two sides of the *kafenio* at the top of the square offer a full view of the community as it slowly comes to life.

'Asters Tripoli lost last night – again.'

The men nod in acknowledgement. The line between day and night creeps over the houses, shining on windows, reflecting orange, contrasting with the blue shutters.

Theo comes out from behind the counter with a tiny cup of coffee that is brewed to perfection, bubbles glistening on the top. He sets it down in front of Socrates, who is sitting on his own at one of the circular metal tables. He acknowledges Theo with the slightest movement of the head.

‘Ah, there goes Vangellis.’

A tractor passes the *kafenio* and turns down the side of the square, puttering past the palm tree and the kiosk. The vehicle belches black smoke, emits a series of crunching, grinding noises and comes to a standstill.

‘That’s it, then, the old tractor is finally dead,’ Old Costas observes. The other men agree, shaking their heads and looking down, lips held tightly together. Out in the square, Vangellis has climbed down from his metal seat and is peering at the tractor, scratching his head.

Just a few days later Vangellis marvels at how his new tractor drives so well and is so fast and smooth compared to the old one. The seat is sprung and it is a joy to manoeuvre. It isn’t *really* new, but it is new to Vangellis, and in much better condition than the old one. The man he bought it from obviously looked after it, and the price was a steal for such a good machine.

Vangellis steers the tractor carefully out of his orchard and onto the road that passes in front of Grigoris’s house. At the back there is a short path, which runs through an orange orchard and then the church’s olive grove, and which connects their houses. It is a path worn by time. Vangellis’s and Grigoris’s babas knew each other, as did their babas before them. Now their wives wear the path a little deeper. But it is an untrodden path for Vangellis and Grigoris. Between them there has always been a little competition – nothing strong, just a slightly abrasive quality to their friendship that has kept them at arm's length from each other.

Grigoris is in front of his house as Vangellis passes, lying on his back under his tractor with a tray next to him. A thin black thread of oil is trickling from the engine into the tray.

'Ah, you should get one of these.' Vangellis presses the brake and pats the steering wheel of his nearly new tractor.

'*Kalimera*, Vangelli,' Grigoris greets him cordially, standing and stretching. 'That's a shiny new toy. I'll bet you paid a pretty penny for that!' Grigoris wipes his oily hands on a rag and steps nearer his neighbour to get a better look at his new possession. The paintwork is good, though there are tiny bubbles of rust here and there that show its age. But the engine sounds smooth and even, and there is no diesel smoke to be seen.

'Runs like a dream, starts first time. I struck lucky with this one. What's wrong with your old heap?' He nods at the tractor, the oil now dripping slow drops.

'Ah, could be one thing, could be another. Seems to be eating diesel.'

'Ah, well, that's where I no longer have a problem. They reckon the fuel economy is just unbeatable with these newer machines. Especially this one.' As Vangellis speaks, he stands up on the tractor to make a point of taking a good look at what Grigoris is doing.

Grigoris in turn stands between his work and Vangellis.

'You should get one of these, Grigori,' Vangellis boasts, sitting down again and then shifting about on the metal seat a little. The scorching summer sun has heated it up in just the time he was on his feet. 'Well, best be off,' he says cheerfully, and a cockerel somewhere in the village calls raucously, as if in agreement. He seems to bounce in his seat as he drives.

'"You should get one of these!"' Grigoris mimics his neighbour and waves his hand dismissively in the direction of the tractor, which is disappearing down the lane. 'If they paid me fair and square for the oranges I grow I could buy one of those,' he grumbles. Vangellis is now level with the church, almost at the square where he will turn left towards his own house. 'Unbeatable fuel economy, indeed!' Grigoris goes on. 'He would say the same if it was terrible. If I had a cold, he would have pneumonia, and if I struck oil, he would find gold.'

He continues to mutter to himself as he fiddles with his own tractor. The sweat runs from his brow into his eyes; the day is passing and so far he has achieved nothing. But there is nothing much he can do until the tractor is fixed. His forearms are black with grease and oil and his rolled-up shirtsleeves are grubby and marked.

'Get one of those, indeed! And how has he afforded to get one of those? With the same number of trees as I have, how can he be doing so much better?' He tightens the last bolt and stands again, brushing off the dust from his trousers and leaving oily smudges. He turns the key and uses the jump leads attached to a free-standing battery to splutter the engine into life. Black smoke billows out of the side of the engine. At least it's running now, but it's still not right. Grigoris sighs. He could spend another day struggling with the engine, or he could just use it as it is and get on with the work he has to do.

'Turn it off!' His wife, Lena, comes rushing out of the house. 'Can't you see I have washing on the line?' She waves her hand and flaps her apron to clear the black fumes from in front of her. 'If you want a happy life,' someone once said to Grigoris in the *kafenio* a week or so before he got married, 'make sure you have a happy wife!' He cannot remember who it was, but it is sound advice. He prides himself that Lena is one of the happiest women in the village. He reaches out and turns the key immediately.

'I see Vangellis has a new tractor,' she says, turning to go back into the house. 'How does he manage that?'

Grigoris sits on an upturned orange crate. Sometimes it feels as if life is just one long uphill struggle. This problem with the tractor has dragged on for weeks and the orchards are not tended – everything feels like it is out of sequence and piling up before him.

He needs to clear away the explosion of spring flowers and grasses from under the citrus trees. The weeds were lush and green in May, but now it is August and they have dried and withered. It is a fire risk and it will invalidate his insurance. There is also his pride. He likes a nice neat orchard, something in his life that he can control.

But there will be no clearing of the weeds, no spraying, no turning of the soil up in the top field. In fact, nothing can be done if this tractor does not work properly. He picks up a pebble and throws it at the tractor's knobbly tyre. How has Vangellis managed to get himself a newer tractor? If they were a little friendlier maybe he could borrow it, or they could have bought it together, shared it. But imagine if he could get his hands on it permanently …

'"The fuel economy is unbelievable!"' He pulls a face as he mimics his neighbour again. He throws a second small stone at the old tractor; it is drinking diesel at the moment. He picks up a third, larger stone ready to hurl, but then his eyebrows lift, his lips part and he begins to chuckle. In his excitement he stands and jiggles, hopping from foot to foot. An idea has struck him, and it is the funniest, most cunning, most audacious of schemes! Could it work? Yes! It could!

'What are you jumping around for, like a chicken looking for worms?' Lena comes out with the empty laundry basket and begins to fill it with the sun-dried clothes from the line.

'Oh, nothing.' But he can hardly contain his giggles, and he grabs her round the waist and kisses her. 'The clothes, Grigori,' she protests, but she is smiling too now. The plan he has just thought up is brilliant – genius, even. But he can tell no one. He stifles his laughter and it makes the undersides of his ribs tremor. Not only is it a brilliant idea, but it is going to be fun!

That night he listens for the banging of shutters as the villagers tuck themselves in for the night. The chorus of dogs begins as the cicadas finish their rasping serenades, but otherwise all is quiet. It is still stiflingly hot inside the house and Lena has kicked off the sheet, her face slack, allowing a rivulet of saliva to dribble onto the pillow. Slithering from the bed, he tiptoes to the door, picking up his trousers and shirt on the way. He dresses as quietly as he can, hopping from foot to foot in the kitchen, which is thrown into slatted high relief by the moonlight through the shutters, and sneaks outside.

With a jerrycan of diesel in one hand, he tiptoes down the back path to Vangellis's yard. There won't be any noisy dogs this way. His neighbour's house is dark, with not a light showing, and not a sound. The tractor is there in front of the house, shining dully in the moonlight. Grigoris stands in the shadows outside the gate for a few minutes, alert for any signs of life, and then, when he is satisfied that the coast is clear, he slides with the agility of a cat over to the tractor and, as quiet as a farmyard mouse, he removes the cap from the fuel tank. Then, slowly, quietly, he unscrews the cap from the jerrycan and lifts it up, carefully pouring the contents into the tank until it is filled to overflowing. Once done, he puts everything back as if he had never been there, his soft flip-flops leaving no marks in the dust, and he returns home and slips back into bed. Lena stirs but does not wake.

Despite having got his tractor going after a fashion, it refuses to start the next day, and Grigoris spends another fruitless day battling with the engine. Although he is exhausted, he makes the same midnight journey, to fill his neighbour's tank again.

On the third day, Vangellis passes by as Grigoris is inspecting the glow plugs. He has spent all morning lying on his back under the machine, trying to get the spanner into the right position, and he has skinned his knuckles twice. Vangellis slows down as he passes Grigoris's gate, grinning and bouncing on his metal seat.

'Hello, neighbour!' he calls, obviously very pleased with himself. 'Oh, Grigori, you will not believe the fuel economy I am getting out of this tractor! If I had known I would have traded my old one in for such a machine long ago. You should get one!'

'They are too expensive for me,' Grigoris says sadly, purposely adding a certain thrill to Vangellis's joy by admitting that Vangellis is the richer man.

‘Ah, you have to know the right people,’ Vangellis counters, in what is almost a sympathetic tone.

‘Maybe you do.’ Grigoris is not sure how much longer he can keep himself from laughing.

That night he does not refill his neighbour’s tank, nor the night after.

‘I finally had to fill her up,’ Vangellis says as he passes the next day. Grigoris says nothing, and struggles to keep a straight face.

That night Grigoris fills the tank again, and the night after that. Vangellis is boasting to anyone who will listen about the wonderful performance of his new tractor.

‘You just won’t believe the hours I am getting from that machine.’ His voice has grown louder and it has more confidence as he addresses the other farmers in the *kafenio*. ‘Never known a tractor like it. Unbelievable. Mitso, why do you keep that old Massey Ferguson when you could have one like mine? Theo, it would really keep your costs down when it comes to olive harvesting.’ On and on he drones, and each night Grigoris tops up his tank.

‘It seems to be running better and better.’ Grigoris catches him talking to Vasso when he stops to buy milk for Lena at the kiosk in the middle of the square. Even Lena mentions it when he walks into the kitchen.

'If you got one of those machines Vangellis has, we would cut our fuel bills for the year in half, he reckons – more, even.' Lena is gutting and preparing a fish, the scales all over her hands and on the counter, down the front of her apron, glistening with petrol hues in the summer sun.

By this time Grigoris has given up on his own tractor. He cannot afford to take it to Aleko the mechanic, and he has wasted many days on it to no avail. Vangellis would know how to fix it in an instant, always has been good like that, but he will not give that man the satisfaction. No, he has bigger plans than that, and if, meanwhile, he must dig his land by hand, then he will. Besides, he is quite enjoying the pace of working just with his hands, and he doesn't spend anywhere near as much time in the *kafenio* now, so he saves money that used to be spent on endless cups of sugary coffee. He is feeling fitter, and Lena seems to have noticed too. Certainly, she appears to be enjoying his advances more now his pectoral muscles are tight and his belly is shrinking.

Tonight he will take another little wander, only this time he will suck out some of the fuel in Vangellis's tank. Not all of it, just a bit.

This time, he creeps into Vangellis's yard with an empty jerrycan and a length of plastic tubing. He puts the end of the tubing into the fuel tank and sucks on the other end to get it to flow, then directs the free end into the jerrycan. He spits out the taste of the diesel, but quietly, so as not to attract attention, and siphons out a couple of litres or so.

The next morning he is belching diesel and he considers it prudent to refrain from smoking. But apart from that, he continues with his day as normal, clearing the stones from the olive grove and building up the walls that support the terraces. That evening, Vangellis passes without slowing down.

At midnight, Grigoris sneaks out again and siphons more diesel out of the tank, and the next day when he sees his neighbour, Vangellis's face is drawn and there is no smile.

'Everything all right?' Grigoris asks cheerfully.

'Oh yes.' Vangellis almost chokes on his feigned cheerfulness. 'Just, you know, going to fill her up.' He pats the tractor but there is none of the previous love for his vehicle showing.

The bragging is slowly replaced by whining as Grigoris repeats the same process three days in a row. The men in the *kafenio* either become bored with Vangellis's moaning or have private little chuckles at his sudden change of heart over his wonderful machine.

The next day, as he passes Grigoris's house, he comments, 'It must be the heat, she seems a little thirsty.' It is not so much spoken to Grigoris as to himself.

'Oh.' Grigoris does not trust himself to say any more.

That night, Grigoris all but drains the tank.

The next morning Vangellis comes past his gate on foot. 'Where's your tractor?' Grigoris asks cheerfully.

'Damn useless machine,' Vangellis replies, kicks at a stone in the road and walks on past. But half an hour later he is back again; he hovers outside Grigoris's yard and then finally rests his crossed arms on top of the wall, his chin on his hands.

'So what's wrong with *your* tractor then?' He's trying to sound casual, but the words come out strained.

'No idea,' Grigoris replies – and it's true, he really does have no idea. 'Could be anything. I've changed the glow plugs, and the oil but …' He is ignorant when it comes to machines and he knows it.

'It's always been a reliable machine though.' Vangellis puts his hands in his pockets and walks over to Grigoris's gate.

'Well, if you want to look,' Grigoris offers.

'Let me see, maybe it is something simple.' Vangellis starts poking about, clearly knowing what he is looking for. He is a natural mechanic. 'Ah!' He sounds a little thrilled but quickly covers it with, 'Oh. Oh dear.'

'You can see what it is?' Grigoris asks. But he is not looking at the tractor – he is reading Vangellis's body language.

'Well, no. Like you said, it could be anything.'

Grigories steps back and sighs, but then with renewed animation he turns to face Vangellis.

'Did you find out what was wrong with your tractor?' he asks.

'You know, I called the man who sold it to me, but the number he gave me must have been wrong as there was no answer. So I rang the dealership, you know, just to see if they had come across such a problem before, and they positively laughed at me when I told them how many hours I had been getting for so little fuel. They treated me as if I was a joke and even put the phone down on me in the end.' Vangellis's speech touches Grigoris, it is so open and honest, but he cannot stop his little game now. He is so close to winning, and he hardens his heart. 'You know what, Vangelli,' he says. 'I think it is going to cost you a lot of money to fix your tractor but I reckon you could fix mine in an afternoon if you really set your mind to it. It is a machine you know well. You have seen it run for years.' He pauses to let this sink in before continuing.

'As for me, I would have to pay to fix mine, or pay to buy a new one.' After a deep breath he says, as if it has just struck him, 'Here's an idea. What if we just swapped tractors? Then you don't need to pay anything at all, if you think you can fix her. As for me, I would be taking a gamble. But a tractor that uses too much fuel is better than one I cannot use at all … What do you think?'

Vangellis's eyes widen as the words sink in. His hands grab for each other, his palms rubbing together. He licks his lips and shuffles a bit from foot to foot, looking for all the world like a child who has just been offered an ice cream. Grigoris cannot resist twisting the knife.

'Of course, I might be being foolish. Maybe it would cost more to repair yours than to buy another one. Maybe–'

'Done!' Vangellis grabs Grigoris's hand and shakes it heartily, pumping it up and down. Then he fiddles with Grigoris's tractor for a minute or two, turns the key, and the engine roars to life. He drives off without making eye contact.

Grigoris watches him go, then strides down the lane with a jerrycan in his hand.

Lena is outside feeding the chickens as he chugs into their yard. The sun glints off the engine hood, and the engine is positively purring as he engages the handbrake.

'What are you doing with Vangellis's tractor?' Lena asks. 'And where is ours?' Her voice is incredulous. The whole village knows of the tension between the pair.

'Not Vangellis's, mine!' he announces.

'Yours?' She does not sound pleased. 'Yes, mine! I swapped it for our old tractor.' He grins now, certain that she will be thrilled, but her mouth is a thin line.

'No good will come of it,' she says. 'That Vangellis is a bully, and whatever scam you have pulled on him, it will not end well.' She stalks back into the kitchen.

Grigoris sighs.

Over the next few days, he takes the tractor up to the olive orchards and makes short work of clearing the stones, hauling away the dead branches, and generally making the farm look tidy. The tractor performs beautifully, and Lena's frostiness disappears. Even Vangellis seems happy enough, although Grigoris sees him once or twice by the side of the road, peering into the depths of the old tractor's engine.

With this new tractor, Grigoris decides, he might be able to take on some contract work and get a little extra money coming in. He has got out of the habit of going to the *kafenio* and he feels he has time on his hands. Yes, this little game with the tractors has worked out very well indeed!

A few days later he returns from a day's work, whistling a tune over the low grumble of the machine.

He turns into his drive and shuts off the motor. 'What's for dinner?' he calls to Lena, and pokes his head in through the kitchen door. Two men are sitting at the table, and they stand as he enters.

Lena does not look happy. The two men are casually dressed but definitely not farmers.

He looks from one to the other, and then at Lena, who folds her arms across her chest. He does not recognise either of the men.

'Are you Grigoris?'

'Yes?'

'And whose is the tractor out there?'

'Mine!' Grigoris rubs his hands down his trousers. For some reason they have started to sweat.

'And the tractor Kyrios Vangellis is using is his?'

'Yes …' He cannot help frowning. These men don't look like farmers or tractor dealers. 'In what way can I help you?' The taller man takes one hand out of his pocket, producing a flash of glinting silver metal and the impression of blue.

'Police. I'm sorry to tell you your tractor is stolen property, Kyrie Grigori. We have to seize it.'

'No!' Grigoris steps outside, towards his beloved machine, and the men follow.

'We have reason to believe Kyrios Vangellis bought it in good faith, but the fact remains the people who sold it to him had no right to sell it. Do you have the keys?'

His mouth hanging slack, Grigoris cannot find words to express what he feels. He points to the ignition. Why him? Why is it always he who ends up worse off? Why?

The shorter of the two policemen fills out a form and indicates where he must sign. The taller one has climbed onto the seat – his seat! He starts the engine and drives Grigoris's tractor, his beautiful red tractor, away. And still he can find no words, no way to resist. Lena comes out, watches the tractor trundling down the road towards the square and rolls her eyes.

As they stand there, watching the red tractor turn in the square and head for Saros town, another tractor comes into view. Vangellis is perched on top, heading towards them.

Grigoris waits to hear what Vangellis has to say about the situation. He will obviously offer the old tractor back. After all, it was Vangellis who made the mistake of buying stolen goods. His old tractor draws nearer, puffing out black smoke, but it doesn't slow down. Maybe the brakes are going too, now. But he can fix that.

But Vangellis is looking straight ahead with no intention of stopping and, as he passes, he briefly turns his head, looks Grigoris in the eye, and grins broadly.

'Bad luck,' he says, and continues on his way.

The Tractor Part II

'That smells so good,' Petros says as his aunt Lena carefully takes the roast out of the oven. There is a shiny new electric oven in the kitchen, but Lena prefers to use the old bread oven out on the patio, round the side of the house, for roasts. It is a large-domed, brick construction, with a metal door at the front and a little chimney that sits at an angle and lets out the smoke from the olive logs that Grigoris cuts and stacks for her. The lamb has been slow-cooking all morning, flavoured with rosemary freshly picked from the garden, and the aromas are amazing. Lena often cooks a leg of lamb when their nephews come to see them, but Grigoris thinks that, this time, their visit may be more than a social call. The boys seem tense somehow.

At this time of year, when it is almost too hot to move and his muscles are relaxed and floppy, it seems difficult to be tense about anything. By the end of August Grigoris has trouble just focusing; the lethargy of his limbs seems to envelop his mind.

Beside the domed oven are three lemon trees that shade the table. Shafts of light fall through the leaves, dappling the smooth wooden surface and creating dancing spots on Petros's and Spiros's youthful faces. They both look like their baba, his brother Karolos, and sometimes he even sees traces of his own baba, their papous, in their features.

Grigoris stretches his legs out under the table. The table can accommodate twelve people with ease. At Lena's name day recently, many more than that were assembled here; it felt like the whole village was in their front yard, and several legs of lamb were consumed that day. But now, with just the four of them, the boys facing him and Lena, it is more intimate, and that is pleasing too.

'So, how's life?' he asks, rubbing his hands together as he watches Lena fill his plate with meat. The vegetables and salad are in dishes on the table. Neither of the boys answers.

'Petro? Spiro?' He looks from one to the other.

'Fine,' one of them mumbles, but as they are both looking down and sitting so close to each other he cannot tell which.

'Oh? What's happened?' Lena takes the lead before Grigoris can open his mouth again.

'We don't want to trouble you with it,' Spiros says, but without much conviction.

Grigoris is about to say something to encourage him to open up, but Lena beats him to it again.

'Your troubles are our troubles.' Her voice is sympathetic. 'So tell us, maybe we can help?' She sets a plate down in front of each of the boys.

'There is nothing to be done,' Petros says, and he sighs deeply. A *chrisomiga* flies into the yard and goes straight over their heads and through the open door into the shade of the kitchen. Grigoris can just make it out as it ricochets off the far wall, flies haphazardly around the room, then bounces off the glazed picture of Lena's deceased parents by the stove that glints as it catches the light. The fat insect narrowly misses Lena's head when it comes buzzing out again, and she ducks and flaps her hand in front of her face. It flies low and Grigoris's attention is caught by little vortexes of dust that swirl and die in the light breeze.

Spiros's expression, which has been glum since he arrived today, at least brightens a little at the sight of the generous portion of lamb on his plate.

Lena helps herself to the salad. She eats meagre portions, in order to 'keep her figure trim,' she told Grigoris once. 'Not enough for a bird,' he replied, though he secretly felt a little ashamed at the size of his own rounded belly. But that was a while ago, and his belly has mostly gone now, as has his jowling second chin. Since he 'got rid' of his tractor last year he has been more active and feels so much fitter. Lena has told him he looks years younger. He is now so active he can eat plates filled to overflowing. He appreciates the benefits to his figure that have resulted from the added manual labour he has been engaged in. That, and he does not have to find money for diesel now.

When he had the tractor, his chores were over so quickly he was often left with idle time on his hands, whereas now he finds he does not have enough hours in the day. His idle hours were often spent in Theo's *kafenio*, and it cost him a small fortune. Now he is physically too far away, out at his furthest olive orchard, to bother about returning to the village for lunch, and so he does without. The ouzo is also a thing of the past as it is not conducive to a full, hard day's work, and so his euros stay in his pocket. When all is said and done, returning to the old ways has been a change for the better on the whole. But his blood still boils at the way Vangelis swindled him out of his tractor. Well, that is not strictly true … It was he who tried to trick Vangelis out of his new tractor, cleverly swapping it for his old one. But it's amazing how Vangelis always seems to come out on top, and it is Grigoris who has ended up with no tractor. It happens every time: Vangelis wins, Vangelis on top, Vangelis comes out best.

These thoughts are unwelcome, and he would like to avoid them, but he glances involuntarily towards the land behind his house. He has an old barn there, and once, a long time ago, when they were on better terms, he gave Vangelis the use of it. Vangelis has stored equipment and fertiliser there over the years, and it has been fine. After all, it is not as if Grigoris has had any real need for the space, and why not help out another farmer? But, as if to add insult to injury, Vangelis now has the audacity to keep the tractor in there – Grigoris's old tractor, the one he feels Vangelis tricked him out of! Only last week Grigoris demanded that Vangelis remove his things from the barn, and they nearly came to blows over it. Vangelis made it difficult, saying he had nowhere else to store his straw and olive nets, fertiliser and plough, as if it was Grigoris's problem!

'Something can always be done about everything.' Lena's words interrupt his thoughts. The heat doesn't seem to make her mind wander as it does his.

'Okay, it's simple.' Spiros speaks with sudden energy. 'It's that Vangelis.'

Grigoris stops eating. The muscles around his jaw twitch; his emotions bubble through as he speaks. 'That Vangelis. What has he done this time?' he snarls.

Lena looks at him, her eyes wide.

'He employed us to build a wall at the back of his yard,' says Petros. 'One to go all around the back and down the side. You know, the old wall that was made of *plythra* bricks. You've seen it, right? The wind and the rain had eroded the mud bricks away, and it was on the verge of collapsing ...'

Spiros takes up the narrative.

'He offered us a job fair and square. To pull down, break up and level off the *plythra* and then to rebuild the wall with concrete bricks and cement and render it.' He nods in his brother's direction for confirmation.

'Yeah, as far as we knew it was a regular job,' Petros says. His fork plays with the fresh salad on his plate.

Grigoris can feel the tension rising in him as the boys voice their grievances. That Vangelis has a nerve! First his tractor, and now this. It's clear from their tone that he has not dealt fairly with the boys. He feels angry. Anything – everything – Vangelis does makes him angry. He has a good mind to go round to Vangelis's house right now, call the old scoundrel out, and threaten to punch him on the nose if he does not make good whatever he has done to wrong Spiros and Petros.

'So, what happened?' Lena asks.

'Well, we did the job, rendered it on both sides, even cleared away the mess, and left his yard as neat as if we had never been there …' Petros says.

'But then he refused to pay us. Two hundred and twenty-seven euros and fifty-eight cents each, to be precise,' Spiros adds.

'What?' Grigoris puts down his fork, and he and Lena stare at their nephews. They are young lads, and they are both honest and hard-working.

'Despicable!' he adds. Lena nods in agreement. The boys will presumably have told their father about it. Grigoris loves his brother dearly, but Karolos is such a passive man that he would rather the boys were cheated than make a fuss.

'Haven't your parents done anything?' Lena asks.

'We dare not tell Mama – you know how she is,' Petros mutters.

He has a point. Nikki is a feisty woman but no man wants a woman to fight his fights.

'You should do something,' Lena says to Grigoris, and the suggestion shocks him. To dream of punching Vangelis on the nose is all right in theory, but Vangelis is a good head taller than him and considerably heavier. The reality is, if the man does not want to pay there is no easy way to make him. And Vangelis is stubborn – always has been, ever since they were boys. At one point, for a brief six months or so when they were at school, he outgrew Vangelis. With the height advantage, it was his turn to do the pinning to the floor when they fought. But, unlike him, when Vangelis's arm was twisted behind his back no amount of force would make him give in. It would get to the point where he thought Vangelis's bones would snap, and Vangelis would suppress little whimpering sounds, but still there was no giving in.

'What should I do?' he asks Lena. 'He is as stubborn as Old Costas's mule!' He shakes his head and his cheeks flush with heat, and he keeps his eyes on his food so he does not have to meet Lena's gaze.

'Ah, but you are cleverer,' Lena says. He glances up at these words, to see Petros and Spiros regarding him with obvious hope in their eyes. He would love to be the hero of the moment for these boys, but he can think of nothing he could do or say that would make

Vangelis pay if he did not want to. He would love to do this to impress Lena, too, but he has lost his tractor and he can't even get his own barn back. The boys do not know the full story, and he cannot tell them all this and dash their hopes.

He makes a sound that implies he is thinking and they continue to eat in silence.

After the meal, Grigoris takes to his hammock by the old donkey shed at the back of the house and begins to doze, trying to suppress his fury at Vangelis. The donkey shed is built of *plythra* too. The mud bricks, reinforced with straw and baked hard in the sun, are an excellent building material, so long as they are rendered and protected from moisture. They provide excellent insulation, keeping the interior of the shed warm in winter and cool in summer.

But, like Vangelis with his wall, Grigoris never got around to rendering the donkey barn, and one side, which takes the force of the prevailing wind and the spring rains, is badly eroded. At some point that wall will be rebuilt with cement blocks. He has even bought the blocks and had them piled in front of the shed, ready to begin construction. The cement blocks are stacked across the entrance to the shed and for the past few months Grigoris has been obliged to climb over them every time he wants to get some tool out or put another away. He must get around to finishing this job. Just as soon as the summer heat cools off.

His eyes close.

He wakes with such a start that he involuntarily grabs at the side of the hammock, which rocks vigorously.

'Lena!' He rolls from his resting place: he has awoken with a plan. He must tell the boys. 'Petro, Spiro.'

Whilst Lena has been tidying and washing the dishes, the boys have been snoozing in their chairs, and they come to with a start at the sound of his voice.

'What?' Spiros is the first to speak.

'I have a way for you to get paid by Vangelis,' he announces proudly, noting the look on Lena's face – she is mystified but impressed. 'Are you prepared to do a day's labour for me for nothing though?'

They frown in unison but soon find their voices. 'Of course,' Petros says. 'As if we would ever charge you,' Spiros assures him.

'Right, then.' Grigoris is about to explain the details of his plan, but a part of him is enjoying the way Lena looks at him, as though he is a hero, and he decides he will keep them mystified for a bit longer. 'Come here first thing tomorrow ready for work, and we will begin,' he instructs the boys, and despite their questions he will say no more about it.

The boys are there just as the sun is rising over the mountains to the east.

'Right,' says Grigoris, with a hand on Spiros's shoulder. 'I'm afraid that, because I have no tractor now, the first part of this job will be the hardest. We will need to take all those cement blocks from here up to the mandarin orchard.' He indicates the pile in front of the donkey shed.

'But that's all the way up the hill,' Spiros complains.

'Well, if you have any other ideas how we can get them to the barn over there ...?'

Petros and Spiros enjoy taking turns to drive their baba's moped up to the barn, pulling behind it an old pram that they have fashioned into a trailer. It does not hold many cement bricks but it is quicker and less effort than carrying them, and a lot more fun, and when they have transported the whole pile the boys are still fresh and eager. They take a couple of bags of cement too.

Grigoris tries not to let his anger show at the sight of his barn full of Vangelis's things.

When he originally wanted Vangelis out of his barn he went to the police about it, at Lena's urging. They showed little interest in his complaints, but they did warn him not to meddle with Vangelis's things, even though they were in his barn. If he were to touch Vangelis's possessions without permission he might be breaking the law, and Vangelis could prosecute. Since he had once said that Vangelis could use the barn, they explained, it made things more complex, and Vangelis had certain rights. They grew impatient with him after that, and it was clear they would not be of any help, so he left.

Well, now he will get the boys' money and his barn back. As for his tractor, never mind! He rubs a hand across his flat belly. Vangelis can keep the tractor and grow fat!

Grigoris peers into the gloom inside the barn. 'There should be some more of my bricks in there. Probably piled up at the back. It's been a while since I've been in here.'

'Is this your plough?' Petros asks.

'No, it's Vangelis's.'

'Vangelis's? So why don't we just take it and sell it? That way we would get our money,' Spiros suggests. He stands in the entrance, surveying the interior of the barn.

'Now, now, boys – that would be straight-out illegal. No, we will be smarter than that.' Grigoris has found the extra bricks and is carrying them, one in each hand, to the barn's entrance. The boys pitch in and soon they are all moved.

'So, there is a standpipe for the water over there, by the gate.' He points to the entrance to the orchard. 'And there should be a pile of sand. Yes, over there. So, boys – to work! I want you to brick up the entrance to the barn, and once it is done, render it, smoothing the edges so it is indistinguishable from the walls.'

The boys are dumbstruck by this request, and neither of them moves or makes any reply. They look at the barn, and then at the tractor, the plough, the canisters of fertiliser and weedkiller, and all the other things stored inside that Vangelis will need very soon – certainly in a day or two – for the tending of his oranges and olives. They turn back to their uncle with puzzled expressions on their faces.

Grigoris laughs at the sight of them. 'Don't you trust your Uncle Grigoris?' he asks, clapping a hand on each of their shoulders.

'Yes, but–' Petros begins.

'But nothing, just trust me. Do as I say, and you will get paid what you are owed, and we will have a laugh too!'

He slaps them both on the back, then wanders away towards his olive groves, where he is in the process of clearing the stones from the soil. The larger stones are used to terrace the hillside, creating retaining walls that help keep the moisture in. His farm has become much neater since he started doing everything by hand. He sees the little things now he is walking rather than sitting atop a noisy, relatively fast-moving tractor.

He clears stones and builds the next section of the wall until the afternoon heat demands that his limbs stop. He will return in the evening when it cools off, but for now he has done enough.

He returns the way he came, past the barn, to find Petros and Spiros have really put their backs into the work. Spiros has found a tall wooden ladder in the barn and is using his trowel to shape a cement block to fit into the last row. Grigoris cannot remember if the ladder belongs to him or to Vangelis. Petros has already begun rendering and is now working at shoulder height. Grigoris shovels sand for the next batch of render, then leans on the spade, watching the boys finish up.

'How's it going?' Lena slices open an enormous watermelon, and cuts chunks of the moist red flesh into a large bowl. Grigoris and the boys attack it hungrily.

'We finished.' Petros sounds proud. Despite Lena's insistence last night,Grigoris did not explain the details of his plan, but he did tell her that the first step was to block up the entrance to the barn.

'Oh, well done! So, Grigori, what happens next?'

'We wait.' He chuckles. The boys join in and so does Lena, but they don't really know what they are chuckling about. They just believe and trust in him and that is enough!

The next morning, before Grigoris is fully awake, Vangelis is banging on his door.

'What on earth do you think you are doing? I use nearly all the stuff I have stored there!' Vangelis is red in the face and sweating, a contrast to the blue sky behind him.

'Well, I did ask you to remove it on more than one occasion.' Grigoris remains calm, in the shade on his doorstep, the sun in his eyes.

'But you cannot just brick it up in there, why would you do that?' Vangelis's face is growing redder and redder, and he looks like an enormous beetroot.

'I can and I have,' Grigoris replies, putting his hands in his pockets, relaxed.

'But how am I supposed to get to my stuff?' Vangelis speaks through clenched teeth.

'Not my problem.' Grigoris jiggles a couple of nails in his pocket. He often finds nails and screws in his pockets, and Lena chastises him, saying that they will damage the washing machine. These are from the other day, when he was fixing the chicken coop.

'Well, I will just tear your wall down then!' Vangelis is physically shaking.

'You could do that. Just as I could have towed your tractor out.' Grigoris is still calm. 'But when I suggested such a thing, what did you say? No, please do not press yourself to remember, let me remember for you. You said that if I were to do that then you would prosecute for any damage I caused. And I seem to remember you saying that you would be sure to find some damage. Now, we wouldn't want any damage to your tractor, would we?' Grigoris is aware that he is goading Vangelis, but he cannot help himself. He feels no fear in confronting this old bully, who has turned a peculiar shade of purple and is wheezing and gasping for breath. Even if Vangelis were to swing for him, and it is a possibility, Grigoris would easily be able to duck out of the way. But Vangelis doesn't make any move. His mouth opens and closes but no words come out.

'But I am not an unreasonable man,' Grigoris continues. 'There is a way you can reclaim your things.' He releases the nails and withdraws his hand to rest it against the door frame, leaning his weight against it.

'What way?' Vangelis's words come out more like a cough.

'Well, you could take the wall down but then, of course, you would have to put it back up, replace it just as you found it. Now, in order to avoid me prosecuting you there would have to be no damage at all. Of course, it would be very easy for me to claim damages. For example, if I thought the brickwork was not as good as it is now, or the rendering not as neat …'

'Oh, come on, man, get to the point. What do you want?' Grigoris has never seen Vangelis so angry, his words spat out, his eyes growing bloodshot.

'Oh, well, it is simple. If you employ the same men to rebuild the wall once you have taken your things out, then I could hardly prosecute, could I? I'm sure the second job will be even better than the first, seeing as they have had practice.'

Vangelis blinks hard several times as he digests this.

'What men?' he finally hisses. Grigoris is having to squint to see Vangelis's face, the sun behind him is so blinding. But he has no inclination to move. He is one step up and therefore has a height advantage.

'Petros and Spiros, and they will be happy to do the job for you for two hundred and twenty-seven euros and fifty-eight cents.' Grigoris watches as the recognition of the exact amount registers in Vangelis's eyes. 'Each,' he adds, and delights in watching Vangelis's Adam's apple bob as he swallows.

'Okay, all right, I see. I am not a fool. I'll pay them – now take that wall down so I can have my tools for work.' Vangelis's shoulders drop, his face sags and he looks like a beaten man as he puts his hand in his pocket and takes out a roll of notes.

'No,' Grigoris says flatly.

'No? What do you mean, "no"?' Vangelis freezes.

'I mean I will not take the wall down.'

'But you just said …'

'I just said you would have to employ Spiros and Petros to rebuild the wall and that will cost you two hundred and twenty-seven euros and fifty-eight cents, each.'

'But you don't want a wall there! That's nonsense! This is just a way to get me to pay, and I have agreed, I will pay.'

'I think they said that taking it down neatly, each brick numbered and ordered so it will go back exactly the same as it was the first time, with no damage done, would be harder. But they are nice boys so maybe they will accept the same as for the build. Two hundred and twenty-seven euros and fifty-eight cents, each.' Grigoris can sense Lena behind him in the kitchen, listening.

'That is robbery!' Vangelis stuffs his money back into his pocket.

'And the taking and using of someone's barn against their will, what is that?'

The money comes out again and Vangelis looks to the sky as he does the calculation, his brows knotting.

'Good God, man, that is nine hundred and ten euros and …'

'Thirty-two cents. But of course there is the cement for the bricks, and the render when you rebuild, so, well, it would be generous to just say a thousand euros all in.

'I haven't got a thousand euros.'

'Oh.' Grigoris does his best to look disappointed as he takes a step back, and he transfers his hand from the door frame to the door, pulling it closed.

'Okay, okay.' Vangelis sounds beaten. 'I'll get it, just get that wall down.'

'Lena.' Grigoris invites his wife out of the shadow of the kitchen. There is a clink, a spoon being left to rest in a bowl, perhaps, and she appears, wiping her hands on her apron. 'Vangelli, I need to hear, in front of a witness' – his hand slips around his wife's waist – 'that you swear on your honour that you will pay if I start the work.' Lena is stiff, but her hip moves against his. It feels exciting.

'I promise,' Vangelis mutters, looking at his feet.

Petros and Spiros only need half a day to remove the wall. Grigoris marks a number on each block, but not in any particular order. Vangelis arrives as the last bricks come down.

'You have the money?' Grigoris wipes his hands on his trousers.

'Not yet.' Vangelis takes the keys to the tractor from his pocket.

'But you have the two hundred and twenty-seven euros and fifty-eight cents that you owe each of these boys. So pay them.'

There is a hesitation. The boys stop what they are doing and stand expectantly. Still with the tractor key in his hand, Vangelis takes out his roll of euros and pays them both.

'And the rest?'

Vangelis is still holding the tractor keys in his fingers, twisting them one way and then another. Grigoris's movement is so quick that it catches him off guard as the key is snatched from his hands. He looks shocked but does not object.

'How about I hold on to the key for the tractor? When you need to use it you can, but until you pay for the rebuilding of this wall, the tractor is mine?' Grigoris says.

Two months later, Vangelis has still not paid the remainder, and so the bricking back up of the barn has still not been done. But this was Grigoris's plan. He and Vangelis have fallen into a routine of sharing the tractor, and the arrangement works well. When they had a tractor each, their machines would sit idle for many days at a time, but now the old workhorse is being fully utilised. They share the cost of the diesel and Vangelis, who likes to tinker, maintains the machine.

There have been other advantages too. Vangelis, having been forced to do much of his work by hand, has lost some weight and his face is no longer crimson with the slightest exertion. Grigoris, on the other hand, is now able to use the tractor for some of the bigger jobs, and can now allow himself a little more time to relax. Lena takes up some of this time. Her hip pressing into his on the doorstep that day was just an introduction to much greater closeness, and she treats him differently now – with respect, and just a touch, he flatters himself, of reverence. Grigoris and Vangelis drink coffee together on occasion, so they can plan out the week and decide when each of them needs to use the tractor.

Now they are talking about sharing fertilisers and weedkillers and other chemicals so they can buy them in greater bulk. That will save a euro or two.

Lena has even suggested that Vangelis and his wife join them for dinner one day next week.

The Desalination Unit

June

It is one of those perfect moments that cannot be expressed adequately in words – that point in the evening when the sun is just sinking to the horizon, turning the scene soft and pink, and painting the few puffy clouds that hang in an otherwise clear sky a brilliant gold. In another few minutes, dusk will be falling, but right now the island could not look more perfect.

From her little balcony on the first floor, Michelle can look out over the port with all its comings and goings, and over the sea to the hills in the distance, behind which the red disc of the sun is now dropping. She could rent out this room at the top of the house, with its sea views, for a tidy sum, but she considers that life is short, so the room is reserved for her to retreat to, in order to put some space between her and the paying guests. Right now, with a glass of chilled wine in her hand and the hotel full, life could not be better. The season has started well, and there is still the summer to come before she will close the guest house for the winter and return to her little house on the mainland, next door to Juliet's. Although island life is blissful, Michelle always looks forward to the complete peace afforded by her cottage in the village towards the end of the summer.

A donkey brays, but it is not one that is in the port. There are only two donkeys visible and she recognises them as Yanni's. He's late to leave for home today. The animals will have spent the day carrying suitcases, people and goods up the narrow alleys of the main town. The cobbled lanes on the island are too narrow for cars or motorbikes, and everything that must be transported is either carried by hand or, if it is too heavy, on the back of a donkey.

The harbour is built in a natural inlet and is more or less square, with wide, stone-paved walkways on each side. The harbour arm, a wide stone jetty reaching out across the mouth of the inlet, almost completes the square, leaving just a narrow opening for the boats to come and go. There is a constant influx of people to the island, which is considered something of an exclusive destination. A daily visitor to the island is the water tanker, a battered commercial ship that brings fresh water across from the mainland. The island's main water source dried up many years ago, and apart from one or two wells there is no fresh water available, and so the tanker comes every day from the mainland, low in the water on the way in, bobbing like a cork when it leaves. The water is pumped high up the hill to a large reservoir that serves all the houses in the town. For quite some time now there have been spasmodic discussions in the *dimos* about installing a desalination plant to relieve the island's dependence on this tanker, but as yet nothing has come of it. Apparently such a unit would transform ordinary seawater into clean, sweet-tasting water fit to drink.

The town itself has been built in the scoop of land above the sea in this narrow inlet. The houses at the harbour's edge are large and square, built of dressed, square-cut stone, constructed over a hundred years ago by rich merchants at great expense. The whitewashed houses behind and further up the hill cannot compete in grandeur, but the view of the houses cascading down the hill to the harbour's edge is dramatic and picturesque. It has brought celebrities and artists here, and many of them keep holiday homes on the island. In the summer it is possible to sit at one of the many harbourside cafes with a retired Greek fisherman on one side and a famous personality on the other.

Michelle takes a sip of her wine and watches the sun disappear and the sea turn inky black. A few orange lights come on around the harbour, casting stripes that ripple across the water.

Yanni the donkey man twists his moustache and rolls a cigarette, fiddling with his lighter, which throws harsh shadows on his features for a moment.

With a click of his tongue, he begins to walk, his donkeys following. Sophia, his wife, will be waiting for him up on the ridge, high above the comings and goings of the town. Michelle loves to walk in the hills and a few times she has found herself up there and has struck up a friendship with Sophia, who is always pleased to have company. As Sophia's belly has grown with their first child, she has become less energetic, and so when Michelle passes by she always asks if there is anything she can do for her. Sophia's answer is always, 'Yes, sit and chat a while.' And so she does.

The last time Michelle was up there – two Sundays ago, was it? – she came back down by a new route, past the dump, a deep ravine that smoulders and burns day and night but never seems to get any smaller. She has been told that in fact it grows each year and is becoming a problem. Apparently, the land either side is no longer used for grazing and is certainly unfit for living on. In short, it has become worthless.

A little memory comes to her now. It intrigued her at the time but she quickly forgot it.

'Dino?' she calls gently through the balcony doors. She can see his naked feet hanging off the end of the bed. He will be reading. Recently, he has become obsessed with the idea of learning to kitesurf, having seen some Americans trying it in the waters around the island. He is convinced it is the sport for him but, as yet, he has not actually had a go.

'Also, when I get reasonable at it,' he said enthusiastically, 'we can offer it as a package to people who stay, lessons maybe, or encourage people who can already kitesurf to stay.' Not that they need more people. The place is already full for most of the summer.

'Dino?' she calls again, a little louder, and this time his feet move.

'You need more wine?' He comes with the bottle and a glass for himself and she moves her feet off the chair so he can sit down. She holds her glass out for a refill.

'Actually, I didn't call you for more wine, but seeing as you are offering …'

'So you just needed *me* then?' He leans forward and kisses her, his lips growing more insistent with every second. Michelle pulls away.

'No, listen. Last time I went for a walk I came down past the dump, and I noticed at the time, but then forgot, I think I saw Adonis down by the water's edge. Then, as I walked further I saw whatshisname, walking quite briskly back to town.' Adonis has been Dino's best friend since birth. The two were very close before Dino left the island, and now he is back they have taken up their friendship again as if no time at all has passed. But Michelle has never been sure if she likes Adonis. Sure, he is tall and eye-catchingly handsome. The rumour is, he has even done some modelling in Athens – but when it comes to Dino he is a jealous friend and has never made Michelle feel she is welcome. Her instincts tell her not to trust him.

'Whatshisname?' Dino prompts.

'Yeah, you know, the guy with the uneven ears.'

‘Oh, the deputy mayor, that whatshisname.’

‘Yes, him.’

‘Hmm. I cannot imagine why Adonis would be down there. I mean, that’s his land, yes, for all it’s worth – but it’s so small it’s good for nothing anyway. Do you think he’d been talking to the deputy mayor? Are you sure? Adonis has no time for politics.’

‘No. There was nothing to indicate they had been together. It just seemed odd. Maybe I was mistaken. Maybe it was neither of them … How’s Adonis’s house coming along, anyway?’

Nearly all the lights have come on around the harbour now. Maybe she should put hers on too. She still cannot believe her luck. It was all in the timing – she had the cash just as the hotel’s previous owner decided to retire – and it could not have gone more smoothly. Yes, she should put the lights on, so the guests will feel welcome when they return from the bars and tavernas. She stands.

‘Where are you going?’

‘To put the lights on.’

He is on his feet before she has finished her sentence.

‘I’ll do it … As far as I know all work has stopped on his house. He is out of money – again.’

‘Is he still with Anastasia?’

‘You know, I think he is serious about Anastasia. I think if his house was finished he would be even more serious. It cannot be easy living in one room with his mama … Just a second.’

He steps back inside, and the thump-thump of his bare feet on the wooden stairs repeats itself after the lights come on and he resumes his seat.

Michelle tops up his glass and the bottle is empty.

‘I wonder if it was the deputy mayor. He looks shifty, don’t you think?’

‘You know what I think? I think you should come inside with me. I think you need a foot rub, a massage perhaps?’ He slips off his chair, his hand sliding to her waist, and it is the most natural thing in the world for Michelle to follow his lead.

Early July

‘How are you?’ Michelle calls. Sophia is shelling peas in a colander on her lap, her feet up on a donkey saddle that has seen better days, and she has not noticed Michelle’s approach.

‘Oh, hello. How’s business?’

‘Great! We’re booked up and there’s still another couple of months to go. You fancy a walk?’

The colander is placed on the windowsill and Sophia slips on her shoes.

'You know, the last time I was here I think I saw something strange down by the dump.' Michelle is no longer sure it was Adonis, or the deputy mayor. It seemed a long way from the town for anyone to be hanging about.

'You can see the dump from here, you know, if you go up on that outcrop.'

They both begin an idle walk in that direction. Sophia walks with one hand on her substantial bump until they reach the summit, then stops and turns. Michelle follows her lead.

'Well, would you look at that!' Michelle exclaims.

A large ship is moored in a bay down past the dump, against a crumbling jetty. There are several men onshore and even from this height they can just hear the shouting as a cement lorry is carefully backed off the tailgate of the ship onto the pier. Michelle and Sophia watch the activity for some time and then walk on around the hill and back to Sophia's house, where they drink coffee and while away time talking about the baby until all thoughts of what they have seen are forgotten.

Late August

A group of men has gathered outside the hotel, along by the clock tower, on the wide harbour walkway. They are suited and look rather serious, and they are shouting at each other.

'What's going on?' Michelle is standing on the hotel steps. Dino has just returned with the sheets from the launderette. The season will be over in another two weeks, and Michelle will not be sad to see an end to the constant task of laundering sheets and making beds for another year.

'It's unbelievable.' Dino puts the sheets on the table just inside the door, knocking a stack of maps onto the floor.

'What is?'

'The *dimos* have brought over a desalination unit and they have installed it, ready to pipe up to the reservoir.'

'Really? They've been talking about that for years, haven't they? Let's face it, the tanker delivering water every day was archaic and probably very costly. It makes so much sense to use seawater instead. So why are they shouting? It can only be a good thing.'

'As if anything ever goes straight, round here.' Dino stands next to her on the steps looking at the crowd of men.

'So what's happened?'

‘It turns out they have flattened a piece of private land and poured concrete on it, without the owner’s permission. That’s what all the shouting is about.’

‘Oh, you’re kidding me!’ Michelle gasps, but then starts to giggle. ‘Actually, why does that not surprise me? So what are they going to do? Can they dig up the concrete?’

‘I doubt it. I imagine it’s pretty thick.’ His arm is around her shoulders.

They stand and watch as the men head down an alley by the clock tower that leads to the government offices.

‘Dino,’ Michelle puts on her seductive voice.

‘What?’ Dino asks cautiously.

‘Go and see what’s happening.’

He doesn’t need to be asked twice. His youth shows as he takes leisurely but quick strides around the harbour edge and then up the alley, following the suited men. Several other local men are following as well. After an hour, Michelle becomes impatient and she too walks past the cafes and into the courtyard around which the town council offices are arranged. The offices are housed in an old Venetian building where Michelle pays her water bill, and which always makes her feel as if she has suddenly stepped across to Italy.

The noise of men arguing leads her to one of the larger rooms, where important announcements are made and court cases tried. Several black-clad local women are hovering in the doorway, as if they dare not go in. But a courtroom used to be Michelle's place of work, before she moved to Greece, and so she strides in with confidence.

She stares and blinks as if the contrast of the sun outside and the shadow inside are playing tricks with her eyesight. But it is no trick. There at the front, on a raised platform, next to the mayor and the deputy mayor, stands Adonis.

She spots Dino, who beckons her to his side.

'You won't believe this! It looks like it is Adonis's land that they used for the desalination unit.' He is grinning.

'Oh! Poor Adonis. And why are you grinning?'

'Listen.' He looks back at the shouting throng.

'My Greek's not good enough, tell me.'

'The deputy mayor is telling the mayor that the fault is theirs and Adonis is saying he wants the unit and all the concrete removed.'

'But I thought you said the concrete would be too thick to dig up.' Everyone is shouting, and no one seems to be listening to anyone else. The effect is a little intimidating, but rather comical too.

'That is what they're saying, but Adonis is adamant. The deputy mayor is almost siding with him, which is odd.'

Michelle recalls the sight she witnessed. Maybe it *was* Adonis on his land, and perhaps it was the deputy mayor she saw walking away. But if that was the case, why has such a thing happened? After all, she saw them – if it really was them, and she cannot be entirely sure that it was – long before the concrete was poured.

There is a sudden strained silence over the men at the front and the crowd hushes. A man in the grey suit has taken centre stage and he is tapping on a calculator. He shows it to the mayor, who first goes red and then blanches.

'He's just calculated how much it would cost to dig up all the concrete that has been laid and remove it,' Dino whispers. The silence does not last long, and soon the shouting begins again, and this time it seems they are arguing over the cost of dismantling the equipment and moving it to another spot.

Then Michelle watches as Adonis cups his hand over the deputy mayor's ear, and the deputy mayor leans in turn to the mayor and speaks earnestly for a few minutes. The mayor nods, and he looks relieved. The mayor then raises his hands and calls for silence.

'I believe we have a solution,' the mayor says.

Late September

Before Michelle leaves the island she wants to say goodbye to Sophia. The baby will probably come whilst she is away and she wants to make sure Sophia has her mainland number so she can ring and tell her the news.

As she arrives, Sophia comes out of her cottage with two cups of cold coffee.

'You know, Yannis's mama and baba still have water in the well,' she says. 'That's pretty unusual for this time of year. It's normally dry by now, like ours. But, come November, the rains will fill it again.'

'Oh, that's nice and cold,' Michelle says, taking a sip of her coffee.

'It comes out like that, ice cold.'

'I take it you heard about the situation with Adonis's land?'

'Oh no. You know what Yanni is like, he just has no interest in other people's business. Which is noble and good, but I do like the occasional juicy piece of gossip, so tell all.' Sophia rests her cup on the curve of her huge belly.

'Well, there was all hell going on about how they would have to remove the concrete slab off Adonis's land, and then up sparked the deputy mayor and – well, the long and the short of it is that Adonis has agreed to rent the land to the *dimos* indefinitely, but because the whole thing was done without his consent they agreed to a price that was way more than it's worth. Half the island is against it and other half thinks the *dimos* has got what it deserved!'

'Oh my goodness! What does Adonis think?'

'I have no idea, but what I do know is that Adonis is no longer building his house with his own hands. No, he is employing other people to do it for him now.'

Michelle stays for a good couple of hours, and then with kisses and hugs she takes her leave for the winter months.

'Call me when the baby comes,' she shouts as she leaves, and Sophia waves the piece of paper with Michelle's phone number on it in reply.

Two days later, the hotel is locked, and Michelle's and Dino's suitcases are waiting to be loaded onto a water taxi and taken across to the mainland.

Adonis comes running, out of breath, and Dino slaps him on his back as he stands trying to catch his breath.

'You going, then?' Adonis asks, a teasing accusation.

'What do you think? You think I want to stay in this godforsaken hole over the winter when the population drops to a handful of locals?' Dino teases in return, and the two shake hands and hug each other tightly.

Michelle looks at Adonis through narrowed eyes. She really does not know what to make of him. They have never really got on. Adonis is so protective of Dino, and he has never been happy about his old schoolfriend being in a relationship with this foreign older woman.

'Michelle,' he says stiffly, and holds out his hand for her to shake.

'Adoni,' she answers, with a cursory shake.

'So, get off my island, you two. But Michelle, I want you to promise something.' he says.

'What?' She does not trust him at all.

'Now I have a house, I can have a wife if I choose,' he says.

'So?' She looks at Dino to see if he understands what is being said, but his face is blank.

'So, promise to come back for my wedding.'

Dino blinks and a slow smile creeps over his face.

'Anastasia said yes!' Adonis confirms, and Dino gives a whoop of joy and slaps him so hard on his back that Adonis staggers forward into Michelle. His face is so close to hers she can see flecks of gold in his dark irises, and before he stands up straight he gives her a very knowing wink.

One Hundred Euros

It is a slow day in a little Greek village. The rain is beating down and the streets are deserted. The men huddle around the pot-bellied stove in the *kafenio*, hands extended for warmth. Theo, the proprietor, looks out across the village square, where the lights of the kiosk cast a warm glow over a scene that is otherwise grey and gloomy. The bakery is closed and the light and life of Stella's eatery opposite is hidden behind the kiosk. Mitsos, Stella's husband, will be running it, but in this weather he will be doing little trade. Theo reminds himself to go over later and pay Mitsos for the ouzo and brandy that he brought back from Saros last week – a month's supply. Theo owes him one hundred euros. But if it keeps raining like this it will be a while before there is that kind of money sitting in the drawer of the old till in the *kafenio*.

Theo is smiley by nature, but this morning a frown clouds his features. No one is paying anyone. Take Aleko, the village mechanic, for example. He has run up a bill of a hundred euros or so at the *kafenio*, with a coffee here and an ouzo there. It's not that he is not willing to pay; rather, that his customers are not paying him. Round and round it goes.

'Hey, Theo, you want your coffee grounds reading?' It is Babis, who has just returned from Saros, where he was defending a group of gypsies accused of stealing goats, in a court case. He spent months preparing and, judging by his jovial manner, the outcome was positive for his clients.

'Not really,' Theo says, gulping down the last of his coffee.

'Well, if you are not having your fortune read they say you can turn the cup upside down on the saucer, turn both saucer and cup round three times – you know, like it is a steering wheel – and make a wish. If, when you take the cup off, the grounds are all clumped together, your wish will be granted. If they are all spread out and in separate piles you can forget it.'

Theo ignores him. Babis always has something to say about something and none of it is ever very useful. Theo stands with his hands on either side of the sink, arms braced. It is embarrassing, and shameful, that he cannot pay Mitsos. Not that Mitsos would ever hold it against him – he wouldn't, no way. But that almost makes it worse.

He is about to immerse his hands in the warm soapy water in the sink when he stops himself and turns the cup upside down, muttering very quietly between clenched teeth. He performs this action with the cup and saucer held below the level of the countertop so that Babis does not see.

Outside, the rain increases its onslaught and the whitewashed walls of the village houses appear grey, the terracotta roofs a dark brown, the tarmac of the road shining under the single street lamp just outside the *kafenio*.

Absent-mindedly, Theo turns his cup and saucer three times and lifts the cup away. The grounds are piled in the centre, a perfect mound; not a single ground sits by itself.

'Ha,' says Theo. 'Old wives' tales.' And he lowers both cup and saucer into the water, watching as the water turns brown.

Once the cups are all washed and stacked neatly to dry, he looks up to see a very shiny car driving slowly up the road from Saros, towards the *kafenio*. The windscreen wipers swish back and forth, sending torrents of water splashing off on either side. Babis has noticed the car too, and his eyes follow its progress. The car turns left towards the church, presumably heading towards Stella's hotel on the beach.

Sarah is on reception at the hotel and Stella is in the office sorting through invoices and orders. Opening the hotel is the biggest and scariest thing Stella has ever done in her life but now, only six months in, everything is beginning to run smoothly. She has the staff she needs and agreements with service providers. Everyone knows that essentially it is a summer occupation, and the bigger businesses, like the laundry, are quite happy to wait till the season starts to get paid. Cash flow problems, Stella tells herself, are a problem for any new business. Next year she will hold back all she needs so she has a float that will take them seamlessly through the winter. It would have been possible, although difficult, to pay all the outstanding bills had the hotel minibus not broken down. Aleko's is not a big business, and he will not be able to wait till summer. The last thing she needs is to become known around the village for being a late payer, so paying Aleko when he has fixed it is not just a matter of pride, but of reputation too.

Right now, only two rooms are occupied at the hotel and she is making no profit. The money that comes in each night from the two rooms is just enough to pay Sarah and the other staff, and she has to make them a priority. A couple from Athens were meant to be arriving yesterday but never showed up. So, unless another guest arrives, which is most unlikely considering the weather, there will be no cash to pay Aleko when he returns with the bus.

Stella sighs. The books are up to date, and the orders she needed to put in are done. Three new bookings have come in today, two for March and one for April, and there are six enquiries for August, so it's a good day really. Perhaps she should ask for a deposit when guests book, to make things run more smoothly. But right now she would settle for a hundred euros to get Aleko off her back.

A hiss of rain against the windows makes her look up, across the car park. A shiny, expensive-looking car is pulling up. She returns to the orders, wondering what she could cut back on during these quiet months.

The murmur of voices filters through from reception. Stella looks up again and wills the person to stay. She hears keys being taken from a hook. That is a good sign, unless they just want to see a room. She doesn't have the self-control to stay put and she is on her feet and opening the door to find out what is going on.

'Ah, Stella.'

Sarah is alone. Stella looks about for the customer but there is no one else in the reception area.

'I hope I did the right thing, but the gentleman who just came in asked me to hold a room whilst they go into Saros to see if they can find anything they prefer.'

Stella shrugs.

'For some reason they insisted on leaving a hundred euros to hold the room, but obviously if they find somewhere else they will want that back.'

'Sounds odd.' Stella watches the clouds roll by and she is sure she can hear thunder in the distance.

'Yes, I thought so too. Anyway, it's there.' Sarah points to the note on the reception desk. Stella puts a paperweight on it.

'Fine.' Just then the telephone rings in her office and she hurries to answer it. 'Hi, Aleko. Oh, you have fixed the minibus – thank you so much. Yes, drop it off when you like. How much do I owe you? One hundred. Okay, see you soon.'

There! She almost promised to pay him as soon as he delivers, but stopped herself just before the words were out … Maybe Mitsos has had an amazing day and has taken a hundred at the eatery, or even fifty. In fact twenty will do, just to hold Aleko off until she has some more cash. If she nips out now she can probably get there and back before he arrives with the bus.

'Sarah,' she says, 'I am just going to the village, back in half an hour.'

'Okay.'

Sarah is doubling as waitress in the restaurant today, and she has brought out the knives and forks and is polishing them surreptitiously behind the reception counter. As soon as Stella has gone, she takes the cutlery to the dining room and takes her time folding a few napkins.

Whilst she is in the restaurant, which is at the back of the hotel, Aleko arrives with the minibus. He runs in, with a folded newspaper held over his head against the rain, and puts the keys on the reception desk. He is about to leave when he sees the hundred-euro note on the desk.

'Cheers, Stella!' he shouts through the empty hotel, and pockets the note, leaving his receipt in its place under the paperweight.

If he dodges through the orange orchards and the olive groves he will avoid most of the rain. It's only a five-minute walk, and Theo is bound to have the stove going at the *kafenio* … A day like this warrants a coffee, and maybe even a brandy chaser against the cold.

'Ah, Theo.' Aleko puts his hand on the proprietor's shoulder. Before Theo has time to react, he takes the hundred euros and presses it into his hand. 'A brandy would be very nice on a day such as this.'

Theo takes the note and casually folds it into his shirt pocket, with a glance at Babis. As he pours a good measure of brandy, he eyes his cup on the draining board and shakes his head in disbelief. Whilst he is waiting for the water to come to the boil for Aleko's coffee he takes a book from under the sink, opens it to the last page and crosses out the line that reads *Aleko – 100.*

'There you go, my friend.' He places the brandy by Aleko, who has pulled his chair as close to the wood burning stove as the other men around it will allow. 'This one's on the house,' says Theo.

It's nice to get out of the *kafenio* once in a while. The men are all content and it will only take a minute to nip over to Mitsos.

'Hey, hey, my friend, a grim day! Are you wet?' Mitsos greets him. The chicken hisses on the grill, the fat catching fire as it drips. At the end of the grill, cooked sausages keep warm by a stainless steel bowl of chips.

'You have any business?' Theo pops his head through the internal door to the small room that houses four tables. The two farmers sitting there nod and grunt their hellos, and Theo grunts and nods in return.

'Roll on spring, eh, Theo?' Mitsos offers him a sausage on the end of his long two-pronged grilling fork.

'No, thanks.' Theo takes the hundred euros and slots it between the old-fashioned keys of the ancient till. 'Here's what I owe you for the spirits.' Then he is gone, running between the raindrops.

Mitsos looks twice at the note. It's not often a hundred-euro note makes its way into the village. Putting down his fork, he wipes his hand on his apron and inspects it. At this time of year it feels like a lot of money, but he is fastidious about the eatery, and the butcher and the fuel man are both paid. ... In fact, everyone is paid except Fillipos over at the bakery. Fillipos's attitude is so relaxed that Mitsos feels he might have taken advantage a little.

Well, he can make amends for that right now.

'You need anything?' He pops his head through to the eatery.

‘Another beer would be nice,’ one of the farmers calls back, so Mitsos takes a bottle of Fix from the fridge. He puts the bottle between his knees to secure it and pops the cap off with the opener that hangs from a rather grimy piece of string attached to the handle of the fridge. He has had to find ways to adjust to having just one arm, and these days it is important to know that things are going to be in their place, like the opener, the grill fork, the tongs.

‘Here you go.’ He puts the beer on the table and looks out at the sky that seems to be clearing. There is a rainbow, too, which appears to rise from Stella’s hotel, or down on the beach somewhere, and it arches right across towards Saros. At the thought of Stella, as usual, there is a pleasant fluttering sensation in his stomach. How has he been lucky enough to have ended up with a woman like that for his wife?

‘Ah, Stella,’ he says out loud, and marches quickly across to the bakery.

The front doors are shut so he goes around to the back and finds the kitchen door ajar. Stheno, the old woman who owns the place, is sitting at the table staring into space, and she starts at the sight of him.

‘Fillipos around?’ Mitsos asks. She is small and frail, her clothes hang off her and she is all bone, so it surprises him, as it does every time, when the old woman screeches at the top of her voice and the sound echoes around the house. After a minute or two, footsteps can be heard, and then the double doors through to the bakery are flung open in a cloud of flour dust.

'Mitso, come.' Fillipos beckons him into the cloud. The old woman is staring at nothing again. The bakery is almost too hot, in sharp contrast to the weather outside. It is heated by an old-fashioned bread oven that burns olive logs. 'I've been trying out some new biscuit recipes,' says Fillipos, indicating a tray on one of the large wooden tables that run along the walls of the bakery. 'Let me know which you prefer.'

He breaks a biscuit in half and steam comes out, and he offers half to Mitsos. He eats the other half himself, chewing thoughtfully, with his head on one side. He smiles encouragingly at Mitsos and hands him another.

Mitsos wipes the crumbs from his lips. 'The second, definitely the second.'

'Yeah, I agree. Does it need more cinnamon though?'

'No, I don't think so.' Mitsos takes the hundred euros out of his pocket.

'If you hang on for a few minutes there will be another batch.'

'Actually I have Socrates and Thanasis over there so I need to get back. I just wanted to get up to date with what I owe for the bread. That's about right, isn't it?' He holds out the money.

Fillipos looks at the note and then goes through to the shop.

'That will take you through till next Wednesday,' Fillipos calls through.

'Okay, see you. Good luck with your biscuits.'

The old woman still hasn't moved, and Mitsos wonders what she does all day as he makes his way out of the back of the bakery. The cold hits him after the warmth of the bakery, and he hurries over to his shop.

Fillipos watches him cross the road and disappear into the shadows. He smiles to himself at his luck. He loves his work, and being up before anyone else, and he loves the creativity of making new biscuits or plaiting the bread for celebrations. The old woman who owns the bakery has lost all interest and Fillipos is given free rein to manage the business as he sees fit. Her husband hardly makes an appearance at all these days. Originally he was just paid a wage, but now, with the help of Babis the local lawyer, he is drawing up an agreement that will allow him to buy the place: a sort of rental purchase agreement that the old couple seem more than happy with. The papers are all but ready to sign, and all he has to do is pay the last hundred euros. And here it is in his hand! He cannot help but give a tiny yelp and jump on the spot. Maybe tomorrow Babis can get the old couple to sign. He says nothing to Stheno as he passes her on his way to the *kafenio*. The woman only seems half there these days. He hopes that won't be a problem.

Babis is sure to be at the *kafenio*. Yes, there he is, sitting at a table that commands the view through the front and side windows, a coffee and an ouzo in front of him. Fillipos enters and Babis extends his arm, but it is not held out for a handshake. No, the fingers twitch, ready to take what is offered.

'Right, then.' Babis pulls out a chair, but Fillipos explains that he has a batch of *kourambiethes* in the oven.

'Can we go ahead tomorrow now?' he asks.

'I don't see why not.'

And with this he is gone, happy to be out of the atmosphere in the *kafenio*, with its stale smoke, and into the rain which is at least fresh.

Babis looks at the hundred-euro note, turns it over. There are a thousand things he could do – needs to do – with this money. The papers are nearly ready for Fillipos; this is the final payment. So this hundred euros needs to take care of some of his debt. Now, what is most important? So much of his time lately seems to have been spent smoothing the path that will take him to the office of deputy mayor – it would probably be a good idea to settle some of those bills. The expense will pay itself back many times over. So the best use of a hundred euros would be ... Actually, the best thing he has done recently has been to take the mayor for a meal at Stella's hotel. He still owes her for that, and he may want to do it again.

He stands and throws a few euros on the table. The rain has stopped and the clouds are white now, and puffy against a bluish sky. A stroll along to the hotel will clear his head of the ouzo and prepare him for the evening, which he will spend finishing off Fillipos's papers.

Outside, the air smells of ozone and biscuits. A couple of dogs run about the square and some children dash out of their houses, eager for freedom. The walk past the church is not an unpleasant one and the sky becomes still clearer as he nears the hotel.

'Hi, Stella,' Babis calls. Stella is pulling out books and papers from behind the reception desk. 'Have you lost something?' he asks, but Stella seems too focused to hear him.

'I can see this is a bad time. I'll just leave this here,' he continues. 'It is for the dinner I had the other day with the mayor. His cannot help his chest puffing out as he says these words.

Stella stops and stares at the hundred-euro note he has put down. It takes a moment but then her shoulders drop and she exhales loudly.

‘Thank goodness,’ she says, and pockets the money.

‘What, did you think I wouldn’t pay?’ Babis asks.

‘Oh no,’ Stella begins, but she does not want to tell him the whole story. ‘No, just a busy sort of day.’

Just at that moment a shiny car pulls into the car park. Babis watches as a man in a sharp suit climbs out and walks into the hotel with the air of someone who has made something of his life. Babis cannot help but compare this man’s appearance to his own – the cut of his suit, the shine of his shoes, the preciseness of his haircut. ‘One day,’ he promises himself, and leaves to go home to work on Fillipos’s papers.

‘I’m very sorry, but I’ve been called back to Athens,’ the man says. Stella takes the hundred euros from her pocket and puts it back on the reception desk. His manicured fingers play with the note’s corners as if it means nothing to him. ‘But I am very interested in the area. It has so much history. I will come back as soon as I can.’

Stella nods. She employs Stheno’s nephew, Vlassis, to conduct tours of Tiryns, Mycenae and Agamemnon’s Tomb for guests in the summer.

‘So’ – he pushes the note towards her and then takes out his wallet from his inside jacket pocket – ‘I would like to book for two weeks … This place will be splendid as a base. Do you have a suite? I will have to work as well so a suite would suit me best. And, if it’s all right by you, I will pay in advance, so I have less to think about. How much would you like?'

The Visit

He has been cleaning all day, and stands back to survey his work; he knows, however, that she will not be impressed. The chipped marble is grey in the sunlight that slants between the branches of the orange trees and through the windows, forcing shafts of light into the room. His mama is not going to look favourably on the house. She will say it is nothing more than a barn, an *apothiki,* and technically she will be right. The house is little more than a dwelling fit for goats nestled into the heart of an orange grove. It feels isolated, but it's actually a very short distance from the sea, and even closer to Stella's hotel, where Loukas works. As far as he is concerned, it is home, and he loves the fact that he can be back within his own walls within minutes of finishing his shift, drifting off to sleep to the sound of the cicadas and the rustling of leaves. He wakes to the sound of goat bells and cockerels crowing, and the shade from the surrounding orange trees keeps the place relatively cool.

In fact, his life could not be more perfect, but he cannot deny the nervousness he feels at his mother's impending visit: she might not see it the same way.

Serving at the beach bar with its palm-leaf roof is such a pleasure it almost cannot be described as work. But how will she see it? A waste of his years spent at college, no doubt. From where he stands behind the bar, he can see the dazzling sea glistening away into the distance in one direction, and the wide sandy beach running all the way to Saros town if he turns his head to look the other way.

And then there is Ellie. Beautiful, funny, quirky, sexy Ellie.

He stops wiping the sink to look out of the window. He was nervous when he first brought Ellie here. She might have told him it was not fit for sheep, walked away – from it and from him. But no, beautiful Ellie ran around the outside, the fingers of one hand trailing against the wall until she reached the door. Then she stood in anticipation, her face glowing, her eyes wide with excitement, and she stepped in as if anticipating a wonderland inside, instead of the earth floor, and the rough, unrendered walls.

'Oh, it's gorgeous!' she exclaimed. 'I love the sink!' and she ran her hands over the old, worn marble and gazed out of the window above it. He stood behind her, his hands around her waist, looking up through the dense leaves to the tiniest spots of blue here and there.

Turning his back on the window now, he looks critically around the room. Together they used mud bricks to build the wall that divides the bedroom from the rest of the space. They painted the walls the palest of blues from a large tin of paint he found discarded in one of the storerooms at the hotel. Stella gave them furniture, too – a sofa, a table and chairs. The dresser came from Marina who owns the village shop, and the little tabletop stove is on loan from Fillipos who works at the village bakery, where Loukas used to work. And the bed – well, that has been the only real expense so far. The chimney was added after they built the wall, using more of the *plythra* bricks from a collapsed building a few fields away. To start with, they made a hole in the wall, hoping the whole place wouldn't collapse. But they worked with enthusiasm and the belief that, united, they could conquer the world. Ellie mixed the mud and he laid the bricks, one on top of another, interlocking them into the wall as he went, building the chimney up the outside of the wall, hauling the last rows up a ladder.

Now the inside of the chimney is baked by the fires they have lit, and the outside is rendered and whitewashed to match the rest of the house and to protect the sun-hardened bricks from the rain in the winter. The whole thing looks like it has always been there, always lived in, always a home.

He blows air through loose lips. How lucky is he! Ellie, the house, the job – it is all so perfect.

Except, his mama is coming from Athens …

The house is one thing, but he and Ellie living together as a couple is another. It feels almost too big to face.

Firstly, Ellie is not Greek. His mama is bound to have much to say about that. He is well aware how she bundles all foreigners into one category in her mind, and he also knows her opinion of female tourists. Maybe, once upon a time, the foreigners' ideas were more liberal than those of the average Greek, but not these days. These days they are just people, like them, no different. They are just looking for some sun, a little relaxation, a friendly face. No, the problem will be the whole Orthodox side of things, as she sees it. He can hear her already.

'You are living with a woman and you are not married?' Then she will cross herself three times. 'You see how already her English ways have driven you from the right path? You are an Orthodox Greek. You were born one and you have been brought up to be one. Yet this girl, in only a few months, has led you so far from the path you know to be true. An English girl! Bah! Why? Why are the Greek girls not good enough for you? Eh? Maybe it is because they will not live with you like heathens?'

She will drive him crazy.

Loukas sits at the rickety wooden table and moves it a little to the left and towards him until it is level enough for the whole structure not to rock.

'Maybe I should broach the subject of marriage with Ellie,' he says to himself, not for the first time. It is not that Ellie does not love him or that he does not love Ellie. He does – oh, how he does.

His eyes glaze over as he recalls her form under the sheets when he came back from work last night. The curve of her hips, the dip at her waist as she lay fast asleep on her side. No, there is no question that he loves her. Did he not ask her to marry him within twenty-four hours of knowing her? But then he did not know her history, and he is not sure how she would react if he were to ask again in all seriousness.

A glimmer of hope lifts his chin, but it sinks again at the thought of all that Ellie has endured. Poor Ellie! There was a scandal when she was still at school, and her name was dragged through the papers. Her teacher was seducing girls in his care, and poor Ellie, too young and innocent to know better, got involved in it all, and thought she was pregnant by him. Thank goodness, that was not the case, but the experience has made the girl understandably wary of relationships.

Ellie's short and unsuitable marriage to this teacher is not the only off-putting thought … It is not that he thinks his mama and baba have had a bad marriage, it is just that – well, they have become so fixed, so stuck. It is as if the two of them in combination make a glue that turns them rigid and everything seems set and unchangeable. He does not want to become like them. For his own sake, and certainly for Ellie's.

The rigidity of his parents' marriage could have been the result of their working and living together in such isolation. Grinding spices all day, every day, in the cellar of their home, with such little natural light and such long hours – it was bound to affect them. But six months ago, the very last order came in for hand-ground spices. As a trade it had completely dried up; the business just would not pay any more.

His mama, probably the more buoyant of the two, recently took a job in a smart new hotel in Gazi, near where she and his Baba live. She makes beds for a few hours a day, a few days a week. For a while, she seemed to change, have more life, more to say, but now his baba has taken a job at the hotel too, as a doorman. Sure, he has learnt to say 'welcome' in six languages, and it gave Loukas hope that his parents would break free of their insular lives, but now the hotel work is all they talk about. Their outlook remains narrow, superficial and pointless. They do not even talk as if anyone else works there, let alone stays there. It is just like grinding spices all over again; they do their work as if it is disconnected from the real world and it seems to fossilise them and segregate them from the world.

Is he being unfair? Probably.

But if he were to persuade Ellie to marry him, is that how they would end up? Insulated in a pointless existence, confirming to each other over and over that the way they are living their life is all right, when really they are just in a rut?

He takes up the broom to sweep the floor again, but it is spotless.

His mama is coming to force an announcement of marriage: that is the point of her pilgrimage. To put pressure on him to give her the gift that she can display and croon about to the world so that, for a moment, her boundaries will be expanded. That is not a good reason for him to persuade Ellie to marry him, nor for her to agree to it.

He releases the broom and goes to the open door. The cicadas are almost deafening here in the heart of the orange groves. The black-and-white cat that has turned up recently is rubbing itself against the tree stump where Ellie sits to brush her hair each morning, with the sun brightening her tiara of loose, bed-messed, criss-crossing hair as she combs it all smooth.

Married to Ellie! In an ideal world it would not be such a bad thought. In fact, if it could be done in their own way, it would be quite a nice thought. His Ellie, his ring on her finger, telling the whole world that they are together. Yes, he likes that. But then, that dark shadow of the chance of ending up like his parents rears up, alongside Ellie's pain over her mistake of a marriage, and his beautiful dream pops.

Leaning against the door frame, he surveys the bloated oranges hanging heavy on the trees. The late summer rain really filled them out, and the skins are so thick you can peel them with great ease, and they are so sweet! He plucks one from nearest tree and begins to peel it.

If he had some big news to tell his mama, something to distract her from the whole question of marriage, that would work. If he had had a promotion, a really spectacular one, it might keep her mind occupied. But how can you be promoted when you work at a beach bar? 'Up' from there would be working inside the hotel, and he does not want that!

Should he just ask Ellie if they could be engaged for a while to appease his mama? Or is that ridiculous? Maybe it is a practical solution?

Pondering this idea, he wanders in amongst the trees, throwing the orange peel to the ants as he goes.

It is easier to think of nothing in particular, and his mind soon goes blank. His natural tendency is to head for the sea and before long the glimpses of blue become dominant.

Ellie will be home soon. She too works at the hotel, on the reception desk, sharing the hours with another English girl, Sarah. Sarah is good company for Ellie but he cannot help but think Ellie's Greek would improve more quickly if she worked in a Greek-speaking environment. Also, Sarah has a goat herd she looks after and her hours are becoming increasingly erratic. Ellie looked a little pale as she left for work this morning. It could be that the extra hours are too much for her. Yesterday she hardly ate a thing, complaining she felt sick. It could be the work, but then again it is possible that she is stressing over his mama's visit.

He looks at his watch. His mama's bus will be in the village in an hour. Behind him, past his cottage, he can just make out specks of white, the wall of the first whitewashed house at the edge of the village, and beyond that is a lane, and the village square where the bus will stop and his mama will descend with her judgements and her disappointment.

He can't face it. He should have told her not to come. He should have taken the time to explain to Ellie what she is like, what to expect, the pressure the old woman will inflict on them.

Turning back towards the glimpses of sea between the leaves, he spies a movement. It's Ellie, striding across the grass by the hotel, slowing down as she heads between the trees. She is waving. He waves back but he feels no joy. She is moving more quickly, trotting. She must be even keener to see him than usual, if that is possible.

'Louka!' she calls whilst she is still some distance away.

'Hello.' He cannot help but smile in return, her energy is so vibrant. But a frown flickers over his brow. She has dark circles under her eyes.

'Is your mother here yet?' she asks, a little out of breath.

'No, not yet. I'm watching the time though.' He swallows to release the tension in his throat, rubs at his neck and moves his head around in a circle as she passes the last few trees.

'Hello, beautiful.' All his worries just melt away as soon as she is in his arms. Ellie is his sole focus and her lips are soft. But he has not kissed her nearly enough before she pulls away.

'What? What is it?' he asks softly.

'Well.' She holds his hands, creates a space between them. The muscles around his mouth start to twitch. Should he smile? Should he cry? She is going to say something big, he can feel it. 'I suspect that your mama is coming here to push you a little. Am I right?'

He does not know how she knows this. He has not mentioned a word. His mouth opens and closes but he has no idea what to say.

'She wants to see us married and everything to be in its place. Am I right?'

'Yes.' His tongue and his throat allow him the one word.

'So, let's set a date.' She is smiling, her eyes shining, as if she is being naughty, teasing.

'Are you serious?'

'Of course!' She laughs a little as he takes her in his arms.

'Oh my goodness, Ellie, this is wonderful, I am so happy.' All his fears and worries of ending up like his parents evaporate at the thought of being joined to Ellie, man and wife. 'I can hardly believe it. I was just thinking the same thoughts myself before you came. Oh, this is wonderful.'

'It would be more wonderful if you would kiss me.' Ellie lifts her face to him and he obliges.

It is easy for time to stretch out and become lost when he kisses her, and when he finally surfaces he looks at his watch.

'Oh, I'd better go and meet the bus.' He turns to go but then stops. 'What was it that caused you to make such a decision?'

She shrugs, but she has that glint in her eye again, as if she is teasing. He cannot leave his mama waiting though. 'I'd better go.'

He sets off through the trees, but he has not gone far when she calls.

'Louka?'

'Yes?' he calls in return.

'You might also want to tell her I am pregnant!'

The Minister

Babis's hand fumbles for the alarm clock. Opening only one eye, he tries to check the time, to see how long before the alarm will go off. He cannot afford to be late.

'What!' He sits bolt upright in bed, looks again at the clock face and then out of the window at the silhouette of the olive tree against the fading sky. He never sleeps long in the afternoon, so why today? He scrambles to his feet, every movement hurried.

His shirt is pressed and ready and he clumsily pulls it from its metal hanger on the back of the door, and at the same time forces his feet into his best shoes, which he polished earlier and placed by the bed. A splash of cold water rouses him, and he uses his wet hands to smooth down his hair in an attempt to tame his tangled locks. A last check in the mirror confirms he looks a little rougher than he had hoped, perhaps, but he is ready. Half past six. Yes, there is time.

Pushing aside the coats and jackets that hang from the hooks on the back door, Babis rummages for the handle. Every movement is jerky in its haste. He flattens his hand against his breast pocket to check for keys and money, then the door is slammed shut. A muffled sound tells him all the coats have fallen on the unswept kitchen floor, but even if he cared he would not have time for that now.

The village is humming with life in the early evening cool, and the moon is just rising over the tops of the buildings. Down in the square, white-haired men sit with their sleeves rolled up, three or more at each of a dozen or so circular metal tables that are arranged around the central palm tree, across the road from the *kafenio*. Theo, the owner, trots backward and forward across the road, tending to his customers, with a tray balanced on one hand and his halo of frizzy hair bouncing as he moves. Babis takes in all the familiar faces. The farmers congregate here after the sun goes down, when no more work can be done in the orange and olive orchards, and sometimes he joins them.

But not today. Today he turns away from the square on the road out of the village. Stella's eatery is also busy, but then how difficult can it be to fill four tables? She waves to him cheerfully as she clears away used plates. He smiles in return, but the smile turns into a sneer as he crosses the road to his car. Some people have no idea what it's like to do a really important job. Oh, for the luxury of just making a few plates of food a night, or serving a few coffees like Theo.

There are no street lights on the Saros road, but the moon is full and it casts a gentle glow on the orange orchards on either side. The cypress trees, tall and ragged, contrast darkly with the midnight blue of the cloudless sky. Babis rarely smokes, but a cigarette now will calm his nerves. The drive to Saros is not far – just one cigarette – but he uses the time to rehearse what he will say.

'Welcome, Kyrie Lipare, it is with great pleasure … No, no – it is our honour to welcome you … No – it is our esteemed honour …'

Babis arranged the visit. It was he who contacted the minister and invited him to Saros. The mayor of Saros does not even think along these lines; he just stumbles along, concerning himself with local matters and never thinking any bigger. Well, he, Babis, the 'Lawyer for the People', will make his mark. The deputy mayor has been there for years and will be soon retiring – why not get a younger man in? It's about time some young blood had an influence.

'Concentrate,' he encourages himself. 'So – we start by welcoming Kyrios Liparos …' Or perhaps it is better to talk to him as an equal: 'Your visit is a good opportunity to exchange ideas, to move our relationship forward.' Babis rolls down the window to let the cooler night air in, and the aroma of jasmine fills the car as he passes a low-lying cottage surrounded by blooms. Should he have had a bouquet of flowers ready in case the minister brings his wife? Perhaps, but the shops are shut so it's too late now.

The Minister for Small Business and Entrepreneurship, coming to Saros town, at his request! This is just the sort of thing that will keep him in people's minds further down the road, when, one day, he runs for mayor. 'Mayor for the People' sounds even better than 'Lawyer for the People'.

Babis rattles the car over a series of potholes to park by the harbour's edge. Another example of the mayor's lack of concern for the townspeople. Does he not know how much he would ingratiate himself with the public if he filled in these holes?

Angelos and his boys had better have done their job well. A good first impression, that's what he needs to make on the minister today. It cost him every penny of his savings. He has cleared out his bank account, and with just a twinge of conscience smashed the ceramic piggy bank he had had since he was a boy, which always sat on top of the fridge in the kitchen. He even went through the pockets of his winter coats for loose change and took out a small loan on his credit card. But if Angelos has done a good job it will be worth all that and more. If all goes well, the mayor, the town, even the minister, will never forget him. His name could be bandied around parliament up in Athens. Maybe even the prime minister will be told of him. Ha! He has invited the local TV station, and if the spectacle is impressive enough, who knows, perhaps it will appear on the national news! He does not want to chase the possibility away by thinking it, but he knows that this is what he is banking on.

The warm night air soothes his worries as he walks with a spring in his step to the town hall. It is a grand old house that was built by a wealthy shipowner in the nineteenth century and has now been converted into offices for the mayor and other local government officials. As he nears the building, he can see men bent over, setting the fireworks in place. Surely they should be finished by now?

'Everything all right?' Babis is aware of the tension in his voice as he addresses the nearest worker.

'Eh?' the man answers, straightening up and fishing in his shirt pocket for his cigarettes.

'The fireworks, they are ready, yes? He is due here in ten minutes.'

'Who is due?' The man lights up and inhales deeply.

'Where is Angelos?' Babis looks around for the man he paid, who is in charge of the whole set-up. He has promised a cascade of white outside the office building, followed by powerful rockets that shoot high in the sky and explode with a satisfactory crack and light up the whole sky. Three minutes of pyrotechnics was all he could afford but the impression should be splendid. He puts his hand in his trouser pocket and jangles the loose change, a handful of euros that must last him until his next paying job. He has three whole *spanakopitas* in the freezer so at least he can eat for the next week or so. There is Angelos now, leaning against the wall, chatting.

'Ah, Angele, everything good? Babis asks, trying to sound cheerful. People are gathering, wondering what is going on. The more the better, as far as he is concerned. Let the whole town see what he is doing, who he is. Where is the TV crew?

'Yes, fine,' says Angelos. 'Actually, more than fine. I've added in some extras between the first set and the rockets, to make the transition more spectacular.' Babis cannot control his instinctive reaction, and a frown passes across his brow.

'At no cost to you,' Angelos adds hastily, and Babis's frown turns into a smile. He slaps Angelos heartily on his back and turns to see the mayor coming out of the impressive tall double doors of the town hall.

'Ah Babi …' The mayor looks a little perturbed. 'What is all this?'

'This,' Babis announces with a sweep of his hand, 'will put us on the map.'

'Put *you* on the map more like.' The mayor is a straight talker.

'If it leaves an impression on the minister it will do you no harm either,' Babis replies sullenly. The mayor has no idea of the personal expense he has incurred to make this happen.

'So where is he?' the mayor asks.

'Five minutes.' Babis looks at his watch. He nearly sold that too, to afford this dramatic greeting. A crowd is beginning to gather, aware that something is happening. Angelos is talking to a small group, and pointing at Babis.

Babis stands tall and his chest puffs out. In ten minutes' time his will be the name on everyone's lips. He will outshine the mayor and all his cronies.

The mayor lights up a cigarette, but does not offer one to Babis. Not that he wants another cigarette, really. Having made a concerted effort to become a smoker, he never quite got the hang of it – but it would have been nice to have been offered one. After all, they are on the same team, are they not?

'Is that him?' The mayor points with his cigarette at a black Mercedes that is approaching. It has an Athenian number plate. The car is new and shiny and looks distinctly out of place, and could not be carrying anyone but the minister.

'Now!' Babis hurries over to Angelos, who has begun chatting to a couple of young girls. 'Now!' Babis shouts. 'Light it now, he is coming.'

Babis is beside himself. The fireworks must be lit as the minister steps out of his car so as to make the maximum impact as he walks up the road towards the town hall.

'Give me two minutes,' Angelos says. 'It's no problem, we will have them working in two minutes.'

No problem! How can Angelos sit there and calmly state that there is no problem when they have been over this countless times. Did he not make it clear that the fireworks needed to be ready for the minister, without fail? No wonder nothing works properly in this parochial little town, with attitudes like this!

'Now, Angele!' Babis shouts. 'There's no two minutes for you to finish up! It has to be now!' Sometimes the only way to get through to these people is to shout, make a fuss and stir things up a bit. His outburst has drawn the sort of attention from the onlookers that Babis would usually do anything to avoid, but there is no time to worry about that now. At least it has had the desired effect on Angelos, who is now shouting at his workers.

Babis looks down the street to where the Mercedes has parked. The back door opens, and a shiny shoe descends onto the pavement. This must be the minister. Where are the fireworks? 'Right,' puffs Angelos, back at Babis's side and looking a little stressed now. 'We are ready. Shall I light it?'

'Yes!' shouts Babis. 'Light it! Light it now!'

The minister is out of the car and is starting to walk up the street. Should Babis have been there to greet him as he got out of the car? No, better this way, let him enjoy the spectacle undisturbed, and be there to meet him on the steps of the town hall.

The first of the fireworks takes Babis by surprise, and draws murmurs of appreciation from the sizeable crowd that has now gathered.

The display begins with a cascade either side of the double doors, raining onto the pavement, little sparks bouncing back up to meet those coming down. It is more beautiful than Babis had hoped and he breathes a heavy sigh of relief. His money has not been wasted. He looks at the faces in the crowd, smiling, or with mouths open, hands pointing. The minister, in his dark suit, has stopped walking up the road and is watching the fireworks along with everyone else. He will have the best view from where he is standing.

The transitional fireworks that Angelos threw in for free are just as wonderful, and then the rockets start, drawing gasps from the crowd. They whizz and whistle into the sky, lighting up the square in front of the town hall in reds and greens and purples. Each rocket explodes with a loud bang into globes of stars, each of which in turn fizz and crackle as they burst again into glowing embers that spiral into extinction.

As the last hiss dies, the crowd cheers and claps and the mayor looks at Babis. Is that awe he sees in the mayor's face – or a little jealousy, perhaps?

The minister resumes his steady pace towards them and Babis readies himself for the accolade.

'Impressive,' the minister says in his Athenian drawl, and he holds his hand out.

'Thank you.' Babis shakes the man firmly by the hand. 'Just a little token of our esteem for our colleagues in the capital. Now, if you would like to follow me, I'll see if we can find you a cup of coffee before we begin. I'm sure you must be in need of some refreshment after your journey.'

'Ah, yes, very kind,' says the minister, and slaps Babis on the shoulder. That's a good sign. They are clearly going to get along well. Babis glances around to see if he can spot the TV cameras. Yes, there they are, trained on his group. That will look good! The visit has got off to a great start, with no hitches so far, and Babis feels sure the hardest part is over. They say that first impressions count, and it is clear the impression he has made is first-rate. Great things will doubtless stem from this. He steers the minister up the steps into the town hall. The mayor is two paces behind. One of the secretaries is hovering uncertainly just inside the entrance, and she stands to one side to let the entourage in.

'Ah, Evgenia,' Babis calls to her. Is that her name? Does it really matter? She is only a secretary. 'Now then, my girl,' he continues, 'how about a cup of coffee for the minister?'

'Er …' the minister mumbles. The woman looks a little confused.

'Greek coffee?' Babis says to the minister. 'Yes, two Greek coffees,' he continues, addressing the secretary now. 'Please bring them up to the mayor's office.' Babis turns around and spots the mayor. 'Better make that three coffees,' he says.

'Er,' the minister starts again. 'I think there's been some confusion …'

'Oh,' says Babis, 'don't you want a coffee?'

'Oh no, it's not that. It's just that … You do know I'm not the minister?'

Babis freezes. Not the minister? But the Mercedes, and the sharp suit, the polished shoes. If he is not the minister, then who is he?

'No,' the man continues, 'I am his assistant. The minister is travelling separately with his wife, and he asked me to let you know that he will be a few minutes late … I hope that's not too much of an inconvenience?'

The panic that Babis feels must show on his face immediately, because a concerned look comes over the not-minister's face now, and he puts a hand on Babis's arm.

'Don't worry, my boy,' he says kindly. 'The minister will be along in a few minutes, and if the display you have ready for him is anything like the introductory show I just saw, I'm sure you'll get on like a house on fire!'

Lissett Bay

Juliet is lazing full length on the sofa on the patio at the front of her house, reading her emails. Her intention was to go quickly through her mail and then start on the translation that's due in a couple of days, but two of the messages demanded her attention, and all thoughts of work have been banished. Not that the emails themselves were distracting … Well, no, that is not true. One came as something of a surprise, but then, of her two boys, Terrance has always been the more capricious. But when the two arrived together …

With a sigh, she shuts the lid and lets her head drop back against the arm of the sofa. The sun has found its way between the vine leaves that cover the pergola and provide welcome shade in the summer months. She narrows her eyes until the leaves become fuzzy shapes, and focuses on the blue sky beyond.

'Sleeping on the job?' It's Michelle, calling from the gate.

'Pondering.' Juliet doesn't move.

Michelle crunches her away across the gravel drive. At this time of year there are still a few weeds – blots of green amongst the chippings. As the heat increases they will wither to brown then crumble to dust, and the drive will be clear, as if someone has taken the time to maintain it. There are not enough hours in the day to weed, mow, deadhead, work and also relax in the sun sipping a cool drink.

'Frappe?' Juliet offers as Michelle draws nearer.

'Just had one.' Michelle plonks herself on the sofa, squashing Juliet's feet. Juliet squirms to release them, giving a playful kick before resting them on Michelle's lap.

'Are you all ready to go?'

'Sort of. I love it here.' Michelle turns her head and Juliet follows her gaze, across to the old barn next door. Michelle has renovated it to a very high standard, and Juliet's farmhouse is a little rough and ready by comparison. Juliet always feels as if she is being spoilt or having a holiday when she goes over to eat with Michelle and Dino, in the winter months when they are here.

'I can't wait to open the hotel, and I love the island life, but I also love the feeling of being on the mainland, shopping in Saros town, going up to Athens.' Michelle absent-mindedly starts to massage Juliet's feet.

'I can't remember the last time I went to Athens,' Juliet muses.

'Probably the last time you were at the airport.'

They sit for a while in silence and Juliet remembers the emails she was reading.

'Do you know anything about probability?

‘Hmm?’ Michelle is still massaging Juliet’s toes, her head back, eyes closed.

‘I got a couple of emails today that have made me wonder about life. You know, probability, coincidences, serendipity. Fate, even,’ Juliet says.

‘I know that coincidences are not always so coincidental if you look at percentage chances or something. What emails?’

‘The way I’ve been looking at it is, every day I go through my emails and everything is unexceptional, so I suppose that the one time something comes up that seems odd then I think of all the possible causes. But I suppose, by the law of chance, one day something will be odd, so maybe it’s not strange at all.’ Juliet pulls a face, knowing she hasn’t been very clear.

‘I know the percentage chance of two people in a class of thirty having the same birthday is much higher than you would expect, but I couldn’t tell you the maths. Anyway, what’s happened?’

‘It just seems that in all the world it would be very unusual for two people I know to end up in the same place.’

‘What, like you and me, you mean?’ Michelle lifts her head off the back of the sofa as a cat jumps on her knee. ‘Which one’s this?’

‘No.’ Juliet smiles as she speaks. ‘Not like you and me. We kind of planned this, in a way. No, I mean two people who I know but who don't know each other ending up in the same place.' Michelle strokes the cat. 'That one is a new one, with no name yet.' The cat tries to sit on Michelle's knee but ends up on Juliet's feet, moulding itself around her ankles.

'So, what emails?' Michelle nods in the direction of the laptop, inviting Juliet to read.

'Well, the first one is from Terrance.' Juliet opens the computer.

'Oh no, now what? Run out of money again? I thought he had finished his PhD?'

'Nearly – another month. Here it is … "Hi, Mum, I hope everything is cool with you", and so on …' She scrolls down. 'And here is the latest surprise, listen to this. "I thought I should let you know that I'm beginning to wonder if waste management might not be for me. I've been thinking about this for some time. You remember me saying how I met that artist when I was in Peru?"' Juliet looks up. 'Did I tell you he went to Peru? It was sort of a paid job connected with his PhD.'

Michelle nods.

'"Well, she got me thinking. She was so creative, Mum, making these art installations from old guns and weapons that had been confiscated by the police in some drug bust. She made this one piece where the weapons hit against each other, making a kind of music which was disturbing but beautiful at the same time."'

‘That sounds interesting,’ says Michelle.

‘If I were to guess’ – Juliet looks up at the vines – ‘she was also pretty and young. Anyway, he goes on.’ She looks back at the email. ‘“Her work inspired me and made me realise that sometimes the world can be changed without having to be totally practical. Her work made me think, and, I’ll be honest, it shocked me a bit, but it carried such a strong message and I felt such a connection I realised that perhaps waste management is not my final vocation.”’

‘He’s not going to quit before he finishes, is he?’ Michelle sits up a bit and looks at Juliet, who keeps reading.

‘“I will finish my PhD. You, for one, have helped me so much it would be wrong not to, but I’ve made a decision and I really need to express myself artistically.”’

Michelle groans. Juliet’s eyes flick up to look at her friend before continuing.

‘“Gabrielle’s next project is an installation in the Halifax Museum of Contemporary Art, and since I got back to London she has contacted me and suggested that we work together on it. Can you believe it, Mum? Gabrielle Bouchard asking me to help! I cannot believe my luck. She’s already exhibited in London, Venice, New York, and now she wants me to assist her. This is a chance to hit the ground running in the art world.”’

‘Has he ever shown any signs of being artistic?’ Michelle asks.

‘He got an A at A level but at that time he was all about changing the world, and he thought waste management would solve everything. You know how he is.’

Michelle grunts and scratches the cat’s neck as Juliet reads more.

‘“So I wanted to let you know that once my PhD is in the bag I’ll be moving to a tiny place called Lissett Bay. Have you ever been? It’s amazing, I visited last week. It’s so hidden away, the houses clustered under the cliffs, practically touching the sea. It’s almost as if it has its own micro-climate. Apparently it has more hours of sunshine than any other place in Britain, and the least rainfall, so some of the local plants only grow there and nowhere else. The sun shone all day the day I was there and when I returned to London the rain and grey came as a bit of a shock.”’

‘Does he always write this much?’ Michelle asks.

‘No, not usually, so I knew it was going to say something more than his standard “how-are-you-can-you-lend-me-my-rent-money?”’

‘Does he say any more?’

‘He says – and this bit is so unlike Terrance it made me wonder – “The place is almost magical, Mum. People go there to sort themselves out. There’s something in the air that is very calming and I don't think I have ever thought so clearly."' She pauses. 'He then goes on to say it would be lovely to see me and would I like a visit. But really, is he serious? Magical? I wondered if he is just scared now his PhD is coming to an end and he has to get a job or something – but to change tack so dramatically?'

'It sounds to me like a good healthy case of infatuation with this Gabrielle.' Michelle shrugs. 'He'll find his feet, Juliet, don't worry. Maybe he'll get his fingers burnt by this girl. He's never had a really serious relationship, has he?'

'No. Well, not that he's told me.'

'He's not a kid any more, and if it's a mistake he'll still have his PhD. It might just be a rebellious act after all those years of studying. Just let him have his fling. And let's face it, there's not much you can do to stop him.'

'Oh, I don't want to stop him. Oh no, let him fly if he can. Like you say, he can always change his mind and get a job.'

'So why are you worrying?' Michelle lets her head rest against the back of the sofa again.

'No, I wasn't worrying. It was just that his email came the same day as this other one.'

'Oh yes, you were saying – coincidence, or whatever. So who is the other one from?'

‘Aaman.’

‘Aaman? I didn’t know you were back in contact with him!’

‘I was never out of contact with him.’

‘I could do with him now. Have you seen my garden?’

Juliet smiles and grunts – a happy sound.

‘He doesn’t do gardens any more. After his return to Pakistan he got a job, then another, and then he got a position – through his uncle, I think – in a firm in Bradford.’

‘No!’ Michelle lifts her head, turns her full attention on Juliet.

‘Aye, lass.’ Juliet now has to fake the accent both she and Michelle grew up with.

‘Well, I’ll be …’ Michelle fakes the accent too, and they both laugh. ‘So what’s that got to do with Terrance? They never did meet, did they?’

‘No, they never met, which is why it’s weird. Here, I’ll read you Aaman’s email and then you tell me what you think.’

‘“Dear Juliet, I hope you are well and your garden flourishes. I write to tell you of changes in my life. Saabira is taking good care of me, and your namesake, little Juliet, grows every day wiser and stronger. But Saabira is a smart woman and she has decided that she wants to become more educated to take a job. To this end she has applied to a very many courses at colleges and universities and she has been awarded a place at Oxton University, to study psychiatric nursing. When I informed my boss he was very sad to know that I was to leave but he was also very helpful with his many contacts and I am so blessed, Juliet, he got me a position just outside Oxton. It is a smaller firm but the pay is the same. But it is an expensive place to live and I fear we cannot afford to rent anything close by, so we took the train to the coast and found a tiny village that is cheap, and the sun was much stronger there than in Bradford. It is called Lissett-Bay. Do you know it?

'"The reason I wanted to tell you this quickly is that I was hoping you would at some point come home to Bradford and I would once again see you. But as we are moving next month it seems that fate is against this as Lissett Bay is very far from everything and I see the chance of us ever catching up with each other again disappearing. But of course you will always be in my thoughts.

'"Eternally, gratefully yours, Aaman."'

Juliet closes her laptop and waits for Michelle to speak.

'Well, that corner of the world is going to pull you in!' Michelle comments.

'But seriously, what are the odds?'

'I don't know. Probably greater than you think. But it sounds like it could be very handy. You can check up on Terrance without him feeling there is too much focus on him, and you can see Aaman, if you want to, but without the awkwardness of having to stay with him. You know …' She pauses, looking thoughtful. 'Sometimes I think it is just best to accept these little quirks of life as gifts. Don't overthink it.'

Juliet nods noncommittaly.

'So.' A cheeky smile tweaks at the corners of Michelle's mouth. 'Have you booked your ticket to visit them yet?'

ΝΑΝΣΥ
ΑΥ.622

Undying Love

They finished eating long ago but the farmers stayed to chat and drink an ouzo or two. Stella sent Mitsos, her husband, home for a *mesimeri* sleep so when the last of the men filed out, in their dark serge trousers and rolled up shirt sleeves, she was quite alone in eatery by the square.

The empty plates and abandoned knives and forks are scattered across the plastic tablecloth, which has men in red coats, on horseback, riding around the circumference after an invisible fox. She should replace the tablecloths, but somehow she never quite gets around to it. That and when she looks at the faded red coats of the riders, and the twist and twine of flowers that swirl around the next table, she appreciates the patterns all over again, and they remind her of good times she has had, good times her customers have had. Mostly they bring to mind the time when they were adorned with flowers for her wedding to Mitsos and she hasn't the heart to discard them.

Stella stacks the dirty plates and cutlery and takes them through to the sink behind the grill, and returns with a damp cloth and a spray bottle of disinfectant to wipe down the tables.

She straightens the cloth with the flowers around the edge, sprays it and wipes it clean. The next is slightly newer, in blue gingham, and then there is the one with large faded flowers in the middle, and finally she wipes her favourite one, with the riders in red coats.

There is a bulge under this last tablecloth, and as she lifts the corner, there, underneath, is a piece of paper folded several times. She is about to scrunch it into a ball when she spots her name at the top, and she pauses to read.

'Oh my.' She wipes her forearm over her brow. For the time of year – early February - the day is uncommonly warm and even in her lightest floral dress she is sweating. 'Oh no,' she whispers as she turns the sheet over.

It is an attempt at a love poem, written in capital letters in a shaky hand. It does not rhyme, nor is it very good, but it is sensitive and gentle, and more than that it is addressed to her.

She tries to recall who was sitting in that place. Surely it was Demosthenes. They were at school together and he taunted her mercilessly, even threatened her once, by the sheep pen up the dry river bed. It seems most unlikely that this is his handiwork. Who else was at that table? Stathis? No, it could not have been him; he is very good friends with Mitsos. Who else? There was Babis the lawyer, but he had an appointment in Saros town and only stayed half an hour. Besides, he is thirty years her junior and rushes around like a baby goat so much of the time he doesn't really notice anyone but himself.

So, Demosthenes! Well that is a turnaround! His tips are always large enough to be noticeable, but love poems? Stella sits at the table and spreads the sheet of paper out in front of her. Mitsos and Demosthenes have hunted together on occasion, and they drink coffee at the *kafenio* together. He was at their wedding, for the love of God! Why would a man do such a thing to another man?

'You still open?' a voice calls from the next room, where the grill is. Stella stuffs the paper back under the cloth and blinks a few times, checks behind her that the tablecloth is smooth and goes through to see who it is.

'*Yeia sou* Theo,' she greets the *kafenio* owner. 'There are a couple of sausages left, or I can do you a *giro*.' She stirs the spoon in the metal bowl of *tzatziki* by the deep fat fryer.

'*Yeia sou* Stella. A sausage sandwich sounds good.' He leans on the counter and plays with a toy car some child must have left.

As she prepares Theo's food the poem plays on her mind. At school Demosthenes was a thug - there is no other word for it - and his picking on her hurt all the more as he was a fine featured boy. Despite his weathered skin and greying hair he is still a not unattractive man, but his ways were always coarse and they turned his pleasant face into something dark and ugly. But this poem reveals a side to him that she did not know he possessed; a subtlety and a delicacy that she thought was beyond him.

'Hey, how much sauce?' Theo laughs and stops playing with the miniature yellow truck.

She looks down at the two sausages on the thickly cut bread that are awash with her home made tomato sauce.

'Oh, sorry.' She takes a knife to scrape it off.

'No, it's alright, the finest sauce in the village.' He smiles and holds out the money. Stella twists the sandwich in a wrap of paper and hands it to him and with a little wave of the package by his ear he steps back into the sunshine. Once he is gone she sets about cleaning the place, washing the pots, sweeping the floor, spraying water on the road outside to keep down the dust and only when all is straight does she collapse into a chair looking out across the square. In less than ten minutes she has forgotten about the poem.

It is only when Demosthenes comes in for chicken and chips again the next day that she recalls the poem and she feels embarrassed that she left it where she found it. Mitsos is by the grill turning the sausages and keeping an eye on the chips. Behind the grill is a narrow space with the sink at the far end and it is here that she goes now to wash up. There's not much; a couple of knives she used earlier, and a chopping board. Once they are washed she wipes down one of the shelves where they keep the glasses.

'Are we not to be served today then?' It is Demosthenes's voice.

'Stella, you there?' Mitsos is shaking the fat off the chips. Wiping her hands on a tea towel she begrudgingly steps through the door to the adjoining room with the four tables. Today Petta, Marina's son, is sitting with Demosthenes. His smooth skin and dark hair contrast Demosthenes's wrinkled features and threads of white hair. Cosmo the postman is also there but he does not order food. His mama has something waiting, and he cannot stay. Thanasis the donkey breeder is at the next table with a newspaper spread out before him. He looks up expectantly as she comes in, and folds the paper.

Stella is sure Demosthenes is looking at her more closely than normal. She shifts her weight from foot to foot and takes their order.

'Three chicken and chips, one with sausages and four beers,' she says to Mitsos, who smiles back at her.

'You alright? You seem a bit fidgety today,' he says.

'I think we need more chips, we are low.' She pulls off her apron. 'I will go to Saros and get some.'

'We have a half bag here ...'

But Stella takes off her apron anyway, and leaves it on the counter. Better to be away, far away. She does not want to be accused of encouraging him.

It's another scorcher. She cuts the corner of the square to take the road up to her house. Their old truck looks for all the world like it has been abandoned. She has no idea how Aleko at the garage keeps it going. Reversing down the drive she swings it out onto the road and then lets it freewheel down to the square where she jumps it into gear and is away.

As she passes the shop she sees Mitsos look up from behind the counter, a smile flitting across his face, but there is also a frown. If he found out about Demosthenes's love poems what would he do, what would he say? But more importantly, who would he blame?

With half an eye on the road Stella searches her memories to try to recall the times that she and Demosthenes have had a laugh in the eatery. On Saturday nights she encourages the farmers to drink ouzo, and turns the radio up so they can sing along. Sometimes they dance. She has not done much of that since she and Mitsos opened the hotel down on the beach, on Mitsos's old onion field. Her Saturdays are now all about organising next week's cleaning, setting up rotas for the bar and reception staff.

She sighs.

'Stationery and staples.' Ellie was on reception yesterday, and she said they had run out of both. Stella can get these in Saros.

She parks by the harbour and wanders into town, and, just for the moment she savours the luxury of forgetting why she is there and looks in windows at high heeled shoes that she would never wear, beaded dresses that are impractical for her lifestyle, and shiny sunglasses that she would be sure to lose. On the road back home she realizes she forgot to buy staples.

Back in the village, Stella parks the truck in the square and hurries across the road to the eatery. Mitsos will be tired, and should go home for a rest. The reason why she left him to run the ouzeri all by himself has to be recalled; Demosthenes has so receded from her thoughts. But when it does come back to mind it also comes with a decision. If the note is still there then he obviously wants her to find it. She will confront him with it, put a stop to this before it gains any momentum. Once it is in the open she will never mention it again, and hopefully neither will he.

'*Yeia*.' She greets Mitsos and dumps the chips on the counter, listening for sounds from the next room, for evidence of Demosthenes. There is no sound of eating or talking.

'Feeling better?' Mitsos asks lightly and then using the tongs he scrapes the bars of the grill, cleaning off burnt fat and chicken skin, that drop into the orange embers and hiss on the coals.

'Why do you say that? There is nothing wrong.' She hears herself snap. 'Sorry, it's the heat. Are you going for a sleep?'

Mitsos comes from around the counter. His apron is not tied at the back and it has curled into a flattened tube, hanging down from around his neck. 'You coming up with me?' he asks, moving closer, looking in her eyes, his hand on her arm, her shoulder, her neck, her ear.

'Maybe I will come in a little.' She smoothes the empty left sleeve of this shirt and tucks it more neatly into his trousers. It is funny to love something that isn't there, but she does. If it had not been for his missing left arm she would not have offered to cut up his food, sat with him over his lunch, talked to him when he had finished eating, got to know him, to love him. 'Yes, I will come in a bit.' She looks him back in the eyes and he places the most tender of kisses on her mouth before breaking free, dipping his head out of his apron and he leaves, whistling.

She watches him go. Age has bent his shoulders over a little, and shocked his hair with white, but time has done nothing to alter the gentleman he has always been. He is the kindest man she has ever known, and he gives her more respect than she probably deserves. He treats her like she is a queen. There are not words sufficient to express how dear to her he is and no Demosthenes is going to cause even the slightest ripple in what she and Mitsos have for each other.

She watches him turn the corner into their road, passing the truck.

With a quick step she is through to the dining room, where she draws out not one but two sheets of paper. The first poem has been worked on and reads a little better. The second is a new one, and it talks of souls and spirits twisting into one. She cannot deny the beauty in the imagery but enough is enough. Would it be better to confront Demosthenes, or tell Mitsos and let him deal with it?

It will be a shame if Mitsos and Demosthenes fall out over this. But Demosthenes is clearly no friend to Mitsos if he behaves like this behind his back. On the other hand, if Demosthenes is just going through a rough patch, perhaps concerned that he is still single at his advanced age, having a momentary fantasy which will pass and embarrass him in a month or two, maybe it is better to just let it burn itself out.

'As if he gave a thought for me when he was bullying me at school!' she sneers out loud, and with this thought she decides she will confront him, make him feel just a little uncomfortable, exact a little revenge. She folds the papers again and pushes them back where she found them.

Tomorrow she will ask him to stay behind after he has eaten and she will pull them out, put them in front of him and see what he has to say. He should squirm.

A light step takes her home for a *mesimeri* sleep, curled up with Mitsos. In the evening she has to go to the hotel to deal with a problem with one of the ovens, but she is back before the eatery shuts. Before they lock up she and Mitsos sit outside under that starry sky sipping ouzo. They watch Vasso close up the kiosk in the centre of the square, and she gives them a weary wave as she turns towards her home. Then Theo closes the *kafenio*, exchanging a few words with the last of his customers, and the village is hushed. All that can be heard is the banging of wooden shutters as people close their homes for the night. Stella and Mitsos sit in comfortable silence as the dogs begin their nightly chorus, no doubt telling each other of the day's events and their hopes for hunting tomorrow. They are particularly noisy tonight and are still going strong when Mitsos suggests they find their own way home, which they do, hand in hand.

The next day Stella feels empowered by her decision to confront her old enemy with the poems. The grill is alight and the chickens on before Mitsos joins her. She has put on a clean apron and tied her hair up. Mitsos always kisses the back of her neck when she does that, and tells her she looks beautiful.

'I think one of the goats, you know the white one with the big horns,' Mitsos rests his chin on the top of her head. 'I think she has a problem with one of her hooves. She is too strong for me to hold, best get one of the young lads in to help so we can trim it.' Mitsos puts his crook behind the door. 'Oh ,you have been busy.' He stands next to her but she does not look up from the charcoals which she is poking about, trying to give them more air. He leans over and kisses the back of her neck and, as always, a little thrill of excitement runs down her spine.

'Hey you too love birds.' It is Fillipos with the bread, still warm from the bakery across the road, and the smell suffuses the air. Stella stops poking the grill to greet him, but her real reason to leave the coals is to pull the end off one of the long baguettes whist it is still hot. The soft, warm middle, torn straight from a fresh loaf takes Stella back to her childhood, helping her mama with the baking on a Sunday morning. It is a safe, nurturing feeling.

'You want a coffee with that?' Mitsos teases, and he stands ready to make one but Stella's mouth is full and she cannot answer. Fillipos grins and leaves, stands by the side of the road for a moment to wait for a grumbling tractor to pass. He nods in acknowledgement to the driver, who is unshaven, with a black cap pulled firmly over his eyes. Two dogs run behind, and the farmer's wife is perched on one of the wheel arches.

'Yes.' Stella finally manages to answer Mitsos's offer of coffee, and she tears off another hunk of bread.

'I'll bring it to you,' Mitsos offers and so she goes outside, pulls out her usual seat and sits in the sun. The village is starting to come awake, with a trickle of schoolchildren wandering into the square. The young ones go to the sandwich shop opposite, buying a *bougatza*, a *spanakopita*, or a *pantofla* and a can of fizzy drink then loiter at the corner where the bus stops. The younger children chat animatedly, but the older ones stand with bleary eyes. When they return it will be other way around. The older ones will be excited, hungry, the smaller children sleepy, ready for their *mesimeri*.

Mitsos delivers Stella's coffee and sits with her as they wait for the charcoal to heat up.

'Oh, I'd better put out more serviettes whilst I remember,' Mitsos says after a few minutes, and he goes inside. A moment later Demosthenes turns the corner on his moped and parks by the kerb right in front of Stella. He makes eye contact and smiles. Stella shifts back in her chair and pulls her skirt down over her knees.

'Looks nice up,' Demosthenes says, referring to her hair. He seems to be expecting a response.

'You're early.' Stella draws her feet in and picks up her drink from the table, holding it with both hands; a barrier between them.

'Ah, just passing by, back later for my lunch.' His tone is cheerful, which infuriates Stella. It is as though he is toying with her.

'Are you not stopping?' Mitsos has come back out.

Stella studies Demosthenes's reaction. Are there signs that he is shocked, or is she imagining it? It makes her smile. Did he come just now not expecting Mitsos to be here this early?

'Just passing by,' Demosthenes says and revs the engine of his little bike and then pootles away, slowly, looking left and right, taking in everything that is going on in the village square.

Later, as the farmers come in for their food, Stella wonders if Demosthenes will make an appearance. He is later than normal and she is surprised to find that she feels a little deflated. A part of her was really building up to facing him with the poems, shaming him.

'It's better this way,' she chastises herself and puts another batch of chips into the hot oil. A group of farmers come in all together as her back is turned. Mitsos is taking orders and serving today as she tends the grill. It is only as the rush begins to wane in the middle of the afternoon that she recognises Demosthenes' s laugh. He must have come in when she was busy with the grill. She does not feel as brave as she did earlier and wonders if facing him is the best thing to do.

'Don't be a coward,' she tells herself and pours lemon sauce over a plate of chicken and chips.

Half an hour later the farmers trickle out. Wiping her hands roughly on a towel and with gritted teeth, she goes through to the dining area. Mitsos is collecting plates and Demosthenes is sitting at the table where the poems are hidden.

'A word before you go, Demosthene.' It's not a question. Before he has a chance to reply Stella collects the dirty plates and the empty bread baskets and takes them back through to the grill area.

'You go Mitsos, I'll finish up.'

'I cannot leave all this to you.'

'I'll be fine, and besides, see if you can't find someone to take a look at the goat before *mesimeri*.'

'Oh, good idea. But are you sure ...'

'Just go! I'll be fine,' Stella replies, and he slips off his apron, takes up his crook and steps into the glare.

Only Demosthenes and a couple of other farmers are in the dining area, and they are making signs that they are getting ready to leave.

'So, Demosthene ...' Stella begins. The two other are almost out of the door.

'Ah, yes. How can I help you Stella?'

She steps up to his table.

'Demosthene, come on.' Thanasis, his fellow diner, reappears around the door frame. 'Kick off it in two minutes. Argentina against Greece.' This last piece of information is directed at Stella.

'Is it now?' Demosthenes looks at his watch. 'Oh yes, you are right. Oh Stella, can it wait?' But he does not expect an answer, and is through the door to the grill before she can respond. Stella watches the pair saunter across the road, laughing. Thanasis's hand is on Demosthenes's shoulder.

The plastic cloth crinkles as she lifts it, and sure enough there are now three sheets of paper. He is gaining confidence. The latest poem talks about 'forevers' and 'never being parted' and also refers to 'being completed' by her and there is some very delicate, thoughtful imagery that touches her more then she would like. The first poem has been copied out neatly and the rough version is no longer there. She cannot help but read this poem through again. It strikes a chord with her and she swallows hard.

Tomorrow, without fail, she will put an end to this.

But when tomorrow comes, despite her careful timing, she is thwarted again, this time by Demosthenes's maiden aunt coming in looking for him.

'Ah, you are here, are you!' the aunt begins as she climbs the steps up into the eatery. Her voice grates, as though it could strip the paint from the chairs.

'My sink will not drain, and he promised to fix it a week ago,' she tells Stella, who tries to smile. 'I don't know how long you think I can live like this?' The old woman is through to the dining area now. 'These are not the days of the Ottoman Empire now you know.'

Her voice grows more raucous and shrill. 'We do not live like heathens now.' She adds a little laugh, as if she is trying to make a joke of the matter but it comes out without merriment. Demosthenes is quickly on his feet and out the door, his aunt trailing behind him, her slow tread following his quick footsteps. The other farmers leave shortly afterwards.

No sooner is the place empty then Stella's hand retrieves the love poems, cautiously, as Mitsos is through by the grill. As she expected now there are four. The last one describes being in her arms and is so personal she can feel the heat growing in her cheeks. She doesn't read all the way to the end before stuffing the sheets back under the cloth. She clatters and bangs the remaining plates and cutlery to cover her embarrassment. He has overstepped the mark. What if Mitsos had found them?

Mitsos always likes to rise at dawn, or before, to take the goats out to graze before the sun is up, and then he wanders down into the village. Today he opens the eatery early, before the village is awake. Later, as Stella enters, she notices that he has picked flowers on his way down from the road side and has put them into an empty beer bottle on the counter. All the jobs that are usually waiting for her are done, and a frappe is on the counter for her.

'I have the feeling that you have been just a little out of sorts recently,' Mitsos explains, adding more charcoal to the grill. It is not the easiest of jobs with only one arm.

'Here, let me do that.' Stella rushes to his aid.

'No, I am fine. You take a rest. Maybe you have been overdoing things?' He finishes with the bag of charcoal and folds over the top to put it under the counter next to the accounts book.

'I am fine,' she replies, but the truth is she is not fine. One poem could be put down to a bit of silliness, perhaps. Two might suggest a bit of a pattern that needs sorting out but three? How is this ever going to end well? It would be gossiped all around the village within hours if anyone were to catch her confronting Demosthenes. It would look like she was withholding what she knew from her husband. But even if she confronts him and she is not caught, she and Demosthenes will then have a shared secret, which would be even worse than the hidden poems. At least right now he does not know that she knows. But if she does not confront him and he keeps going where will it end? Perhaps it would be better to tell Mitsos after all, just give him the poems, let him decide what to do. But then she will be the one to create a problem between her husband and Demosthenes . What if, God forbid, Mitsos sees her showing him the poems as something negative and he sides with Demosthenes? She would have no idea what to do then.

'You don't look fine. Here, coffee, take it outside. Or why don't you go home, have the day off?'

'I' m fine, I tell you,' she snaps and immediately twists her mouth, screws up her eyes. 'Sorry, I didn't sleep well.' She was awake most of the night, turning the situation around in her head, with no solution coming to her.

'Sit, drink.' He waves her out, but before she goes outside she steps around and behind the grill. An old cardigan hangs from a nail in the wall, and a cotton bag someone once left and two baseball hats. Stella feels in the pocket of the cardigan for her cigarettes and takes mixed pleasure in lighting up outside.

'Thought you'd given up.' Demosthenes pulls up on his moped and kicks down the stand. He has a something in his hand covered in a black bin bag, which he takes inside with him. Stella can hear the two men chatting inside. Mitsos's voice is the softer. Demosthenes is laughing. How dare he!

'Right!' She abandons her coffee, stands erect and marches in to face the men.

Demosthenes is still laughing, but more quietly now.

'Mitsos!' She grinds her half smoked cigarette out in the nearest ashtray.

'Stella!' he replies. The black bin liner is on the table and with his one hand he tries to unwrap the contents. Demosthenes steps forward to offer help but Mitsos waves him away.

'I can do it,' he says quietly.

Something tells Stella to close her mouth, wait a moment. Mitsos struggles until finally, with a jerk, the bag falls away and on the table is a large bunch of roses and babies-breath intertwined and sheathed with cellophane. He picks them up where they are tied into a bunch and holds them out her.

'For you,' he says. Demosthenes has stepped sideways and is now slipping out of the door behind her.

Stella can only stare as she takes the beautiful blooms. But once Mitsos's hand is free it is under the table cloth, the riders in red coats taking the hills and the valleys created by the interference in their stride. The sheets of paper are withdrawn and Mitsos holds them in front of him and starts to read.

He reads with feeling, making eye contact with her again and again. When she has finished her says simply,

'I wrote those for you my love. Happy Anniversary.'

Map of The Village

PAPA'S
JELLO
KYRIA SOPHIA
GARAG
CHURCH
MARINA'S
CORNER SHOP
THEO'S
CHEESE FACTORY
KYRIA GEORGIA
MICHELLE'S
JULIET
FRONA'S
MARIA
COSMO
POPPY
PHARMACY
KIOSK
BABIS
SHEEP PENS
BAKERY
LOUKAS & ELLIE
HOTEL
STELLA'S EATERY
SPIROS
TAKIS
NIKI
KATERINA
DORA
YORGOS
SAKIS
ANNA
THANASIS DONKEY BREEDER
AAMAN
MITSOS
STELLA
LIZ & NEVILLE'S

Map of Orino Island

SOPHIA'S HOUSE
YANNI'S HOUSE
PINE TREES
MONASTERY
TOWN
DUMP
KORIFI
RALLOU'S HOUSE
SHIPS ROCK
COVE
CAVE
BOAT YARD
ATHENS
THE VILLAGE
CONVENT
THE HOTEL
SAROS TOWN
SAROS HARBOUR
ORANGE ORCHARDS AND OLIVE GROVES
N
S
E
W

Foreign Phrases Used in the Books

Adio – Goodbye.

Aemmoragia – Hemorrhage

Afiste – Leave it

Agamisou – A profanity. Very rude.

Agapi mou – My love.

Anteri – Cassok.

Apagoreftiko – When the weather is too rough, the port police will stop ferries and other commercial vessels from leaving the port. This is an *apagoreftiko*.

Apo Augousto xeimonas – A Greek saying that literally translates as 'From August it's winter'. The end of August is said to mark the end of the summer, and although it's not unusual for there to be thunderstorms towards the end of the summer, the weather can often be very pleasant indeed right up to Christmas…

Axiopistia – Reliability / trustworthiness.

Apostolnik - An item of clerical clothing worn by Orthodox Christian and Eastern Catholic nuns. It is a cloth veil that completely covers the head (except for the face), neck, and shoulders.

Apothiki – Store room

Baba – Dad.

Baklava - A rich, sweet pastry made of layers of filo filled with chopped nuts and sweetened and held together with syrup or honey.

Balami / Balamoi – A gypsy term for non gypsies.

Barbounia – Red mullet.

Bougatsa – A sweet pastry, typically eaten for breakfast.

Bourtzi – An island fort.

Bouzouki – An eight stringed instrument used in most traditional Greek music.

Briam – A dish made with mixed roast vegetables.

Briki - A small pot designed specifically to make Greek / Turkish coffee. The body and handle are traditionally made of brass or copper.

Chopal – (Urdu) A community building or space in the rural areas of North India and Pakistan.

Chrysomiga – Rose beetle. A beautiful golden-green beetle, rather a clumsy flier.

Christos Anesti – An Easter greeting, literally translated as 'Christ is risen'. Generally followed by 'Alithos anesti' – 'In truth he is risen'.

Daskala – Teacher

Den birazi. Ola kala – It doesn't matter. Everything is ok.

Den eimaste kala – An expression of amazement, similar to 'You cannot be serious!'

Diavatirio – Passport.

Dikigoros – Lawyer.

Dilitirio – Poison.

Dimos – Town Council

Dodeka evro – Twelve euros.

Dolmades – Stuffed vine leaves.

Dyo evro – Two euros.

Efharisto – Thank you.

Eisai Endaxi? – Are you OK?

Eisai kala? – Are you well?

Ela – Come.

Ela do – Come here.

Ela tora – Come now.

Elektrologos - Electrician

Ellinikos kafes yparxei? – Is there any Greek coffee?

Ena Duo – One Two

Ena moussaka, mia salata – A moussaka, and a salad.

Episis – Likewise

Esy fige – You leave.

Ela, pame – Come, let's go.

Etsi ki'etsi – So so.

Exoume – We have.

Fakelo – Literally translates as envelope. Also used to refer to a bribe, presumably because the money is passed in an envelope.

Feta – A tangy Greek cheese.

File – Friend.

File mou – My friend.

Filotimo – Filotimo is considered to be the highest of all Greek virtues which determines and regulates how someone should behave in their family and social groups. It is mostly about respect and doing the right thing. In its simplest form it means "doing good", and it ensures your behavior will make you stand out from others. It will demonstrate what kind of a person you are and the manner in which you were brought up. Filotimo to a Greek is essentially a way of life.

Flying Dolphin – The commercial hydrofoils that serve the islands close to Athens are referred to as Flying Dolphins because of the way they appear to leap over the waves.

Fournos – Bakery

Frappe – Iced coffee.

Frontistirio – Cramming school. Most school children will go to private schools in the evenings to get extra tuition in one or more subjects. School is very competitive in Greece, with relatively few university places available.

Fylakio – A prison in the north of Greece, near the Albanian border.

Gamoto – An expletive. Very rude.

Geia sou – A greeting, used when meeting or parting.

Gifti / Giftisa – Gypsy.

Gigantes – A dish made with butter beans. Tasty!

Giro – A particular kind of souvlaki. To make giros, pieces of meat are placed on a tall vertical rotisserie, in the shape of an inverted cone, which turns slowly in front of a source of heat, usually an electric broiler. If the meat is not fatty enough, strips of fat are added so that the roasting meat always remains moist and crisp. The rate of roasting can be adjusted by varying the strength of the heat and the distance between the heat and the meat, allowing the cook to adjust to varying rates of consumption. The outside of the meat is sliced vertically in thin, crisp shavings when done. It is generally served in an oiled, lightly grilled piece of pita, rolled up with various salads and vegetables.

Glyko – Sweet.

Gymnastirio - Gymnasium

Hasapiko – The butcher's dance.

Hero Poly – Pleased to meet you

Horis kremidi – Without onion.

Horta – Boiled greens. Traditionally collected wild from the mountains, there are many varieties, and they are generally prepared by boiling, and served with olive oil.

I tyxi tis tsiganas – Cocktail invented by Loukas. The name translates as 'The gypsy's luck'.

Ikanopiimeni - Content

Ilithia Anglitha – Stupid English woman

Kafenio – Café

Kala – Good.

Kali Anastasi – An Easter greeting, literally translated as 'Good resurrection'.

Kalimavkion – A stiff, black, cylindrical hat worn by priests.

Kalimera – Good morning.

Kalinixta – Good night.

Kalo kathistiko – The 'best' sitting room. Reserved for guests and formal occasions

Kalo Ximona – Happy winter.

Kaloriziko – Literally translates as 'good roots'. Used to convey good wishes when someone buys a new house.

Kalos orisate – Welcome.

Kanenas – Nobody.

Kastana zesta – Hot chestnuts.

Kataifi – Similar to baklava, kataifi is a sweet pastry made with shredded filo, nuts and honey.

Kefi – Joie de vivre.

Kendrikon – A café in the main square in Nafplio.

Kifissias – A train station in the north of Athens.

Kokkino – Red.

Kolokithia – Courgettes / zucchini.

Komboloi – Worry beads

Koufetta – Sugared almonds, commonly given as a gift to guests at a wedding or baptism.

Koulouri / koulouraki – A bread ring, covered with sesame seeds, usually eaten for breakfast.

Krasi – Wine.

Kyria – Mrs.

Laiki – Farmer's market.

Lefko – White.

Loukoumades – A kind of doughnut deep fried and usually served dripping with honey.

Maayun -

Mageireuo – I'm cooking.

Malaka – An insult. Rude, but commonly used.

Mali Grias – Candy floss. Literally 'Old woman's hair'.

Mana mou – My mother.

Mangas – The streetwise 'hard guys' of Athens, particularly Piraeus

Meleti Meli – Cocktail invented by Loukas.

Melitzanaki – Baby aubergines preserved in a sugar syrup. Generally offered to visitors with coffee.

Mesimeri – Afternoon.

Mesimeriano – Siesta.

Metrio – Medium.

Meze – Hors d'oeuvres.

Mia Beera – A beer.

Monastiraki – An area of central Athens, close to the Acropolis.

Moschari Kokkinisto – Beef stew in a tomato sauce.

Mountza – A rude hand gesture.

Mumija –Mother. (Albanian)

Moussaka – A baked aubergine (eggplant)- or potato-based dish, often including ground meat, with many local and regional variations.

Miaoulia – A celebration held on the island of Hydra in July. Miaoulis was an admiral in the Greek navy, and helped lead Greece to independence.

Nekros – Dead

Nai – Yes.

Nato / Natos – There it / he is.

Ocka – Dad. (Czech)

Ohi – No.

Ola endaxi – Everything ok.

Ola kala – All is well.

Olympiakos – A popular Greek football tea.

Opa – An expression of joy, used particularly when dancing.

Orthayopiskos – Sun fish.

Ouzeri – An eatery where hors d'oeuvres and drinks are served.

Ouzo – A popular Greek spirit, distilled in copper stills and flavoured with aniseed.

Ox Aman! – A Turkish expression of amazement, commonly used in Greece.

Palyatzis – Rag and bone man.

Panayia / Panayia mou – Literally 'Mother of God'. A mild expletive.

Papous - Grandfather

Parakalo – Please / You're welcome.

Parea – Company.

Pastichio – A baked pasta dish including ground beef and béchamel sauce.

Papas – Priest

Patates – Potatoes.

Perimene – Wait.

Pethera – Mother in Law

Pio poli – More.

Plenis ta piata – Wash the dishes.

Pos paei? – How's it going?

Pos to lene? – What's it called?

Psila – Loose change.

Psomi - Bread

Putana – Prostitute.

Plithra – Mud brick / adobe. In the villages, and even in some towns in Greece, houses were traditionally built of large blocks made of a mixture of earth and straw, dried in the sun. The technique was used until at least the middle of the 20th century, and is a low cost and environmentally friendly building material which offers good insulation, and protection against earthquake damage – useful in areas like Greece that are prone to earthquakes.

Pentozali – A traditional dance from Crete

Poios einai? – Who is it?

Pos paei? – How's it going?

Psaltis – Cantor

Re gamo… - An expletive (very rude!)

Rebetika – Urban Greek folk music, almost always featuring the bouzouki.

Regina – A three-wheeled tractor, common in rural Greek villages.

Rizogalo – Rice pudding.

Roma – Gypsies.

Saganaki - In Greek cuisine, saganaki is any one of a variety of dishes prepared in a small frying pan, the best-known being an appetizer of fried cheese.

S'agapo – I love you.

Scordalia – A garlic dip.

Seira sou – Your turn.

Siga siga – Slowly, slowly.

Signomi – Sorry / excuse me.

Sirtaki – Zorba's dance.

Skata – Crap.

Souvlaki - A popular Greek fast food consisting of small pieces of meat and sometimes vegetables grilled on a skewer. It is usually served in a pita sandwich with garnishes and sauces, or on a dinner plate, often with fried potatoes.

Spanakopita – Spinach pie, often made with feta cheese, but traditionally just with spinach

Spiti – House.

Stamata - Stop

Stefani – Crown. Used in a symbolic way in a Greek wedding ceremony.

Stifado - Rabbit or hare stew with shallots, vinegar, red wine and cinnamon. Beef can be substituted for game.

Stin Athina – In Athens

Stin ygeia – Cheers. To health.

Sto kalo – Literally 'Go to the good'. Used in parting.

Strema – A unit of land area equal to one thousand square metres.

Tamata – Votive offerings used in Greek Orthodox churches. Tamata are usually small metal plaques, which may be of base or precious metal, usually with an embossed image symbolizing the subject of prayer for which the plaque is offered.

Tapsi – An oven baking tray.

Taverna – Restaurant.

Taverna tou Kapetaniou – The captain's taverna.

Tavli – Backgammon.

Templon - A feature of Byzantine churches consisting of a barrier separating the nave from the sacraments at the altar.

Ti? – What?

Ti egine? / Ti ginetai? – What's up?

Ti ginetai edo? – What's happening here?

Ti kanei o Markos? How is Markos?

Ti kanete? – How are you?

Ti leei? – What's up? / What's going on?

Ti ora fevgi to leoforeio? – What time does the bus leave?

Ti thelete paidia? – What do you want, guys?

Ti thelis? – What do you want?

To fagito einai etimo – The food is ready.

To ftiaxnoun – They are mending it

Tsapa – A digging tool shaped like a pick axe but with just one wide blade.

Tsangaris – Cobbler

Tsipouro – A spirit similar to ouzo.

Tsoureki – A sweet bread, usually eaten at Easter.

Tyropita – Cheese pie. A popular snack.

Tzaki – An open fireplace.

Vevea – Of course

Voeithia – Help

Yia mas – Cheers!

Yia / Yia sou – Greeting (hello / goodbye)

Yiaourti – Yoghurt

Yiayia – Grandmother.

Ypomoni - Patience

Zaharoplasteio – Patisserie.

Zemra ime – My heart. (Albanian)

Zeybekikio – A traditional Greek dance

Cast of Characters

The following abbreviations are used to indicate which book(s) the characters appear in:

IG – The Illegal Gardener

BB – Black Butterflies

ENOF – The Explosive Nature of Friendship

GD – The Gypsy's Dream

ABH – The Art of Becoming Homeless

MPT – In the Shade of the Monkey Puzzle Tree

HOP – A Handful of Pebbles

TUM – The Unquiet Mind

WWB – Eatching the Wind Blow

RB – The Reluctant Baker

EL – The English Lesson

PW – The Priest's Well

ASATOT – A Song Amongst the Orange Trees

SB – The Stolen Book

RCL – The Rush Cutter's Legacy

Aaman (IG, ENOF, GD)– A Pakistani man who travelled to Greece illegally and ended up living in the Greek village, looking for causal labour. Protagonist in The Illegal Gardener. Later he returns to Pakistan, and we meet him again in Saving Septic Cyril – The Illegal Gardener Part II.

Abby (GD, ASATOT) – An English girl who travels to Greece and ends up in the wrong town. With little money to get to her intended destination, and a storm that thwarts her plans, she takes a job at the eatery in the village, and ends up staying for the summer.

Abby's Dad (GD) – Bernard

Adonis (ENOF) – Mitsos younger brother.

Adonis (ABH, EL) – Dino's childhood friend. Tall, handsome, athletic and charming. But also fiercely defensive over his friend Dino.

Agnes (SB) – Maid in the hotel in the UK.

Aikaterina (MPT) – An Albanian woman who lives in the basement of the second house that Theo rents in Athens.

Aleko (TUM, PW) – A fisherman on Orino island. Sada's husband. Sada is Sophia's sister, and Sophia is one of the main characters in The Unquiet Mind.

Alex & Liz (GD) – Run a cupcake shop in Saros.

Alyssia (EL) – Toula's daughter. Toula is the protagonist in The English Lesson.

Anastasia (Tasia) (MPT) – Girl who Theo meets in the kafenio in Athens. A fiery character, who knows her own mind. We first meet her in In the Shade of the Monkey Puzzle Tree.

Andreas (MPT) – Kiosk owner in Athens.

Andreas (ASATOT) – Sakis' manager, who is much more motivated by wealth and fame than Sakis. Sakis is the protagonist in A Song Amongst the Orange Trees.

Angeliki (TUM) – Sophia's sister. Sophia is one of the main characters in The Unquiet Mind.

Angelos (WWB) – Irini's son. Irini is the protagonist in Watching the Wind Blow.

Anna (BB) – Eleni's girlfriend. Eleni is Marina's daughter.

Anna (ENOF) – Girl in the travel agent's in Saros town.

Anna (ASATOT) – A woman in the village.

Anna (RCL)– Spiros's mother, deceased. Spiros is one of the main characters in The Rush Cutter's Legacy.

Anna Vissi (BB) – A well known Greek singer.

Antigone (ASATOT) – A friend of Sakis' Baba who lives in Piraeus. Sakis is the protagonist in A Song Amongst the Orange Trees.

Antonis (ASATOT) – Antigone's husband, a friend of Sakis' Baba who was considered to be a *Manga*. Sakis is the protagonist in A Song Amongst the Orange Trees.

Apostolis (EL, SB) – Toula's husband, who doesn't pay her much attention. Toula is the protagonist in The Enlish Lesson.

Argyro (RCL) – Spiros's stepmother. Runs the taverna on Orino island. Altogether not a very nice woman. She has become bitter thinking that the way he dowry was lost was unfair. Spiros is Vasso's boyfriend / husband.

Aris & Katerina (ENOF) – A couple in the village, who met as a consequence of one of Mitsos's and Manolis's schemes. Aris mends tractors, and they have ten children.

Aris Karnidiotis (BB) – Jeweller on Orino Island.

Arnold Braithwaite (ABH) – Head of Dulwater & Marown, the law firm in Bradford where Michelle worked.

Artemis (BB) – Marina's younger daughter. Married and living in Athens.

Artemis (WWB)– Captain Yorgos's yacht, which is hijacked by a pirate in Watching the Wind Blow.

Aspasia (MPT) – Girl in the village with no real grip on reality. The other villagers know her and look out for her.

Augustinos (RCL) – Argyro's father. Owned a kafeneio on the harbour front on Orino island. Argyro is one of the main characters in The Rush Cutter's Legacy.

Aunt Efi (BB) – Marina's aunt, who accompanied Marina to Orino when she was a teenager.

Babis (TUM, WWB, RB, PW) – A lawyer who lives in the village. He is full of drive and energy and tends to be single minded, and consequently often does things without regard for others. He is cousin to Yanni the donkey man who lives on Orino Island.

Becky (RB) – Ellie's school friend. A bully. Ellie is the protagonist in The Reluctant Baker.

Bernard (HOP) – A friend of Torin's on the Isle of Man. Torin is an important but relatively minor character in A Handful of Pebbles.

Bibby (TUM) – Hectoras's mule.

Bill and his wife (not named) (BB)– American tourists.

Bob the dog (MPT) – Margarita's mother's dog. Later Theo's dog and friend. Margarita is Theo's second landlady in Athens.

Bobby (BB, ABH) – Kyria Zoe's brother in law.

Bobby (ASATOT) – A gypsy boy in Saros town.

Brian (RB) – Marcus's colleague and boyfriend. Marcus is Ellie's teacher and later husband, and Ellie is the protagonist in The Reluctant Baker.

Brian (SB) – Taxi driver in the UK.

Bun bun (WWB) – Angelos's cuddly toy (a rabbit). Angelos is Irini's son, and Irini is the protagonist in Watching the Wind Blow.

Captain Yorgos (WWB) – Operates a charter yacht out of Saros harbour. The boat is hijacked in Watching the Wind Blow.

Cheri (IG, TUM) – Thomas's girlfriend. Thomas is Juliet's son. Cheri works in finance.

Christopher (RCL) – A man on a yacht on Orino island.

Constantinos (ABH) – Fisherman who supplies Costas Voulgaris's taverna on Orino island.

Constantinos (SB) – Manages the water board office where Niki gets a job. Niki is the protagonist in The Stolen Book.

Cosmo (ENOF, MPT, PW, SB, RCL) – The village postman, and school friend of Mitsos and Manolis.

Costas (BB, WWB) – A young man who helps out in Marina's shop.

Costas – Sakis' Baba, known as Costas the crocodile killer. Sakis is the protagonist in A Song Amongst the Orange Trees.

Costas (SB) – Katerina's husband. Katerina works in the water board office in Saros.

Costas Voulgaris (BB, ABH, TUM) – Café owner, hotelier and philosopher on Orino Island.

Crystal (RCL) – A woman on a yacht on Orino Island. Christopher's wife.

Cyril Sugden (ABH) – One of Michelle's clients when she was at Dulwater & Marown. We meet Cyril again in Saving Septic Cyril – The Illegal Gardener Part II

Damianos (MPT) – Theo's friend from school, now in America.

Damianos (HOP) – A man in the village.

Damianos and Old Maria (TUM) – Two villagers who have decided to sell their houses because of reports that the properties in the village unsafe.

Gerasimos (TUM) – A lawyer based in Saros. Babis' rival.

Demosthenes (GD) – A bully who abused Stella at school but who is now older and wiser, and leaves generous tips when he eats at her eatery.

Demosthenes (WWB) – Port Police Commander in Saros town.

Despina (ENOF) – A kind old lady in the village.

Dierk (WWB) – Irini's mother's brother in law. Irini is the protagonist in Watching the Wind Blow.

Dimitra (MPT) – Theo's mama, loving , kind, maternal.

Dimitri (MPT) – Manager at the Diamond Rock Café in Athens where Theo works. A very shifty character.

Dimitri (RCL) – Spiros's friend. Spiros is one of the main characters in The Rush Cutter's Legacy.

Dino (ABH, EL) – A young man who grew up on Orino, but then moved to the village. One of the main characters in The Art of Becoming Homeless, where he has completed a degree in England but is now dissatisfied with the idea of long working hours and the high cost of living.

Dolly (ABH, TUM) – one of Yanni's donkeys. Yanni is a donkey man on Orino Island.

Dora (ASATOT)– Thanasis the donkey breeder's sister.

Doreen (ABH) – Secretary at Sloughlow & Grotchett who is very chatty with Michelle and tells her all the gossip.

Dr John Brooks (IG) – Juliet's college tutor / lover.

Eleftheria (ASATOT) – One of Sakis' cats. Named after a well known Greek singer, Eleftheria Arvanitaki. Sakis is the protagonist in A Song Amongst the Orange Trees.

Eleni (BB, ENOF) – Marina's eldest daughter.

Eleni (MPT) – Wife of Timotheos, a baker in Athens who befriends Theo.

Ellie (RB, ASATOT) – The protagonist in The Reluctant Baker. Ellie is an English girl who leaves home and travels to the village to escape an intolerable situation. She falls for Loukas, who runs the village bakery, but things are complicated... Later she works as receptionist at Stella's hotel.

Emilianos (EL) – A waiter in a café in Saros.

Emily (IG) – Juliet's teddy bear when she was little.

Fanis (ABH) – Dino's childhood friend. An architect.

Fillipos (RB) – Iason's son, who likes to go running in the mornings and dislikes nightlife, drinking and smoking. Iason is a farmer in the village.

Finn (HOP) – Sarah and Laurence's son. 28yrs old. He is opening his own company selling media space to business startups in return for shares. Sarah is the protagonist in A Handful of Pebbles.

Flessas (ABH) – Goatherder on Orino who helps when Michelle gets stuck

Frank (SB) – Con man on the bus in the UK.

Frona (HOP) – An old woman born in the village. Her sons are Sam who lives in the USA, and Nicolaos who has just moved back from Australia where his estranged wife remains. Nicolaos is now in a relationship with Sarah. Sarah and Frona have become friends.

Gabrielle (RCL) – Christopher and Crystal's daughter. Christopher and Crystal are on a yacht on Orino Island.

George (EL) – Apostolis's business partner in Athens. Apostolis is Toula's husband, and Toula is the protagonist in The English Lesson.

George the Greek (SB) – Café owner in the UK.

George the Greek's cousin (SB) – Slum landlord in the UK.

Gerasimos (RCL) – Bank manager on Orino island.

Giaan (IG) – Aaman's elder brother, died in a fire aged eight.

Glykeria (WWB) – Irini's cousin. Irini is the protagonist in Watching the Wind Blow.

Gorgi (MPT) – Gypsy living next door to Theo in Athens. Riya's brother.

Grigoris (SB)– Karolos' brother, a farmer. Karolos is Niki's husband, and Niki is the protagonist in The Stolen Book.

Grigoris Taxydaktylos (ASATOT) – A clarinetist from Thessaloniki. Taxydaktylos literally translates as 'Fast Fingers'.

Gypsies (BB) – In Black Butterflies, a group of gypsies who were selling rugs from their truck, and were conned by Manolis.

Harpeet (IG) – Pakistani man who turns up at Juliet's house right at the end of The Illegal Gardener.

Harris (ASATOT) – One of Sakis' cats. Named after a well known Greek singer, Haris Alexiou. Sakis is the protagonist in A Song Amongst the Orange Trees.

Hectoras (TUM) - A donkey man on Orino island. Sophia's suitor.

Helena (HOP) –Finn's fiancé. She was born in the village but her family moved to Australia when she was young, then America and she moved alone to London. She works as a freelance photographer. Finn is Sarah's son; Sarah is the protagonist in A Handful of Pebbles.

Iason (RB) – A farmer in the village.

Ilias (ABH) – Dino's childhood friend on Orino, water taxi driver.

Ilias 2 (ABH) – Dino's friend in the village, runs a wood merchants, married to Florentia.

Ilias (RCL) – Fisherman on Orino island.

Irini / Rini (BB, WWB, SB) – The protagonist in Watching the Wind Blow, we first meet Irini in Black Butterflies where she is Petta's partner / fiancé. Petta is Marina's son.

Iro & Panayiotis (MPT) – A couple in the village.

Jackie (GD) – Abby's friend from England, who was already in Greece and had arranged the job Abby never made it to on one of the islands.

Jenny (IG) – Juliet's best friend at university.

Jenny (HOP) - A teenager, related to Helena. She loves dogs. A minor character in A Handful of Pebbles.

Jeremy (HOP) – A lawyer in the Isle of Man. A minor character in A Handful of Pebbles.

Jim (HOP) – Helena's father. Helena is one of the main characters in A Handful of Pebbles, in which she marries the protagonist's son.

Jimmy (MPT) – Bar man at the Diamond Rock Café who has made an art out of skimming money from the till into his pocket.

Joss (HOP) – Sarah and Laurence's son, Aged 29yrs. He works in Finance. Sarah is the protagonist in A Handful of Pebbles.

Josh (ABH) – Child on the boat who picks up a cigarette packet.

Jules (ASATOT) – A journalist who sees life much more clearly than Sakis, but instead of using words he uses actions to gently guide his friend to happiness. Sakis is the protagonist in A Song Amongst the Orange Trees.

Juliet (IG, ENOF, GD, ABH, HOP, TUM, EL, SB,RCL) – An English woman who bought a house in the Greek village to renovate after her marriage break-up from Micki. Her soul originally lodged in Greece when taking a rejuvenating holiday with her best friend Michelle, leaving her husband and mother-in-law to look after her newly born twins. She is fluent in Greek and works as a translator. Juliet is the protagonist in The Illegal Gardener, and makes an appearance in most of the other books.

Kaloyannis brothers (BB, RCL) – Two brothers who manage the boatyard on Orino island.

Karolos (SB) – Niki's husband, an orange farmer. A gentle man who accepts life just the way it is. He is grateful for all he has and seldom asks for more. Niki is the protagonist in The Stolen Book.

Katerina (BB) – Eleni's first girlfriend, at school.

Katerina (EL) – Toula's granddaughter – 3 years old. Toula is the protagonist in The English Lesson.

Katerina (ASATOT) – A woman in the village.

Katerina (SB) – Girl who works in the water board office.

King Nev & Queen Helen (RB) – A couple who live in Little Lotherton, a village in Yorkshire where Ellie moves to, and where Cyril lives.

Koula (ABH) – Adonis's mother. Adonis is Dino's friend on Orino.

Kyria Georgia (ABH, SB) – Juliet's neighbour in the village who loves to grow flowers in her garden.

Kyria Katerina (GD) – Lives opposite the church, was a nurse. Suffers from arthritis. Cares for Marina.

Kyria Maria (PW) – A woman in the village who lives opposite the church. A busybody.

Kyria Papadopoulos (RCL) – A woman who lives on Orino island.

Kyria Poppy (RB) – Shop owner in the village. She sells second hand clothes.

Kyria Sophia (BB) – Marina's next door neighbour in the village. Helps out in the shop.

Kyria Zoe (BB, ABH) – Runs a pension on Orino island. Adonis's aunt.

Lambros (MPT) – Tasia's Baba. Tasia moved down from Athens to the village to be with Theo.

Laurence (HOP) – Sarah's husband. Sarah is the protagonist in A Handful of Pebbles. A pilot.

Leni (ENOF) – Adonis' wife. Adonis is Mitsos's brother.

Leonora (MPT) – Girl employed by Dimitri at the Diamond Rock Café who wants to become a model.

Leontia (RCL) – An old woman who lives on the mainland. Spiros stayed with her and she taught him to cook.

Liz (HOP) – Sarah's friend from school. They moved from Ireland to the Isle of Man together but 30 years later Liz moved to London with her husband Neville. Two years later Neville's mother died. Liz had tended her for 24 years.

Loukas (RB) – The village baker who met a girl from the village at university and married her for all the wrong reasons. She died six months later and Loukas was left holding her parents' family business together. He is unhappy until he meets Ellie.

Mahmout (IG) – A Pakistani man living in the village. He tries to befriend Aaman.

Makis (MPT) – Bouncer / DJ at the Diamond Rock Café in Athens where Theo works.

Malakopoulos (BB) – A family from the village who keep goats.

Manolis (BB, MPT) – One of the central characters in The Explosive Nature of Friendship. A farmer. Later Marina's husband.

Marcus (RB) – Ellie's husband and pottery teacher. He delights in being free and experimenting and experiencing in life - no matter who it hurts. Ellie is the protagonist in The Reluctant Baker.

Margarita (MPT) –Theo's second landlady in Athens.

Maria (BB) – Candle maker on Orino island.

Maria (HOP) – A minor character in A Handful of Pebbles. A friend of the family into which the protagonist's son is marrying.

Marina (IG, BB, ENOF, GD, HOP, TUM, WWB, PW, SB) – A Greek woman who runs the village shop. Protagonist in Black Butterflies.

Marinos (MPT) – An Albanian who lives in the basement at the second house that Theo rents in Athens.

Markos (BB, ABH) – Panos' boyfriend. Panos is a hairdresser on Orino Island.

Markos (MPT) – Marinos and Aikaterina's son. Marinos and Aikaterina are an Albanian couple who live in the basement of the second house that Theo rents in Athens.

Martha the widow (MPT) – A woman from the village whose house is destroyed by earthquake.

Meli (BB) – Marina's first boyfriend. Meli literally means 'honey', and it is the nickname Marina gave him.

Melissa (BB) – literally translates as 'honey bee'. Meli's term of endearment for Marina.

Mercedes (TUM) – The new donkey that Yanni buys from Thanasis the donkey breeder.

Michelle (IG, ABH, HOP, EL) – Juliet's friend from childhood, a lawyer in London. Michelle is the protagonist in The Art of Becoming Homeless.

Mick (IG, GD, HOP, TUM) – Juliet's ex husband, no defined job.

Miltos (TUM) – A taverna owner on Orino island. Angeliki's husband. Angeliki is Sophia's sister, and Sophia is one of teh main characters in The Unquiet Mind.

Mimi (ENOF) – Mitsos's family's donkey.

Mimis (TUM) – A the donkey man on Orino island.

Mitsos (IG, ENOF, GD, MPT, HOP, TUM, RB, PW, SB)– A farmer in the village. Protagonist in The Explosive Nature of Friendship, where we follow him through his life from a young boy to an old man. He loses an arm, and later marries Stella.

Mr & Mrs Papadopoulos (MPT) – A couple in the village.

Mr Dimitri (ENOF) – Mitsos' father.

Mr Froutokleftis (ENOF) – A fruit buyer who bought from the local farmers but never paid. 'Froutokleftis' translates literally as 'Fruit Thief'.

Mr Kleftis (GD) – A lawyer. 'Kleftis' translates literally as 'thief'.

Mr Pseftico (ENOF) – Mitsos' bank manager. 'Pseftico' translates literally as 'False'.

Mr Rodgers (GD) – Abby's physics teacher

Mr Socrates (ENOF) – Grumpy man who owns the mandarin orchard by the riverbed.

Mrs Appleton (SB) – Administrator at the university in the UK.

Mrs Eleni (IG) – A woman in Marina's shop.

Mrs Riley (ABH) – Michelle's housekeeper. Her husband is Michelle's gardener.

Mrs Sophia (IG) – A villager, friend of Marina.

Natasha (RB) – Loukas' wife, deceased. Loukas is the baker in The Reluctant Baker.

Nefeli (PW) – A woman who lives in the village and keeps house for the priest. Nefelii is one of the main characters in The Priest's Well.

Nektarios (GD) – A bully who was at school with Stella.

Neville (HOP) – Liz's husband, 68yrs old, 17years older than Liz. Liz is one of the main characters in A Handful of Pebbles.

Nicolaos (MPT) – Greek Australian shepherd. One of the main characters in A Handful of Pebbles. His mother is Frona who moves back to the village and his brother Sam lives in the USA. Nicolaos is in a relationship with Sarah.

Niki (SB) – Originally from Albania where her parents remained until they died, Niki now lives with her family in the village. She and her husband have always struggled for money and Niki's aspirations for her children exceed their means. Niki is the protagonist in The Stolen Book.

Nikiforos (HOP) – Frona's husband, deceased.

Nikos (GD) – A taxi driver.

Nikos (HOP) – Frona's brother, deceased.

Old Costas (IG, ENOF) – A farmer. Owns the barn where Aaman and the other illegals stay. Manolis's father.

Old Odysseus (MPT) – Keeps chickens and grows aubergines on the outskirts of the village, above the riverbed, where mattresses and other debris are dumped.

Old Spiros (MPT) – Ran the last taverna in the village, that closed some years ago.

Panayiotis (RCL) – Greengrocer on Orino island.

Panos (BB, ABH) – Hairdresser on Orino island.

Penny (ABH) – Michelle's sister. They are not close.

Penny (RB) – Ellie's school friend. A bully. Ellie is the protagonist in The Reluctant Baker.

Petros (BB) - Taxi boat man on Orino Island.

Petros (SB) – Niki's son. Niki is the protagonist in The Stolen Book.

Petta (Petalouda) (BB, WWB) – Marina's son. Real name Alexandros Mavromatis . One of the central characters in Black Butterflies. *Petalouda* means butterfly in Greek.

Phaedon (MPT) – Owns the building where the Diamond Rock Café is situated.

Pru (HOP) – Joss's wife. her full name is Prudence but Sarah (Joss's mother) secretly calls her Pruella de Vil. She is 30, born in the US, lived in Hong Kong, London and Douglas and sells software. She is good at her job.

Richard (IG, ABH) – Michelle's husband, a lawyer in London. Michelle leaves him in The Art of Becoming Homeless.

Riya (MPT – Gypsy who lives next door to Theo in Athens.

Rockie (GD) – Abby's dog.

Rudolph (HOP) – A minor character in A Handful of Pebbles. A friend of the family into which the protagonist's son is marrying.

Saabira (IG) – Aaman's wife, lives in a small village outside Sialkot, in Pakistan. We meet her again in Saving Septic Cyril – The Illegal Gardener Part II.

Sada (TUM) – Sophia's sister. Sophia is one of the main characters in The Unquiet Mind.

Sakis (ASATOT)– A singer / songwriter who represents Greece in a song competition and wins, but with a song that he considers musically poor. Following his success at the competition he must decide whether to retain his integrity as a musician, or follow the money and fame. Sakis is the protagonist in A Song Amongst the Orange Trees.

Sam (WWB) – A mercenary who takes over Captain Yorgos's yacht in Watching the Wind Blow. His real name is Peter.

Sarah (HOP, TUM, RB) – The protagonist in A Handful of Pebbles. An Irish woman who comes on holiday to the village, staying at Michelle's holiday let cottage. Whilst there she takes the time to reevaluate her relationship with her husband. Later she gets a job at the hotel and minds a herd of goats.

Savvas (PW)– A priest who gets iinto some kind of trouble in the US and is transferred to the Greek village. Savvas is the protagonist in The Priest's Well.

Sir Sloughlow QC (ABH) – Michelle's boss at the law firm in London (Sloughlow & Grotchett).

Sister Katerina (TUM) – A nun who lives in the monastery near to Yanni's house on Orino Island.

Socrates Rappas (BB) – Priest on Orino island.

Sonia (GD) – Abby's new stepmum.

Sophia (TUM) – A girl who left Orino island after a terrible event and was brought up by the nuns in a convent near the Greek village. She was Yanni's childhood sweetheart before she left the island.

Sotiria (TUM) – Sophia's sister. Married an Athenian and now lives in the US.

Sotos (PW) – A priest in the Greek village (deceased). Savvas' predecessor. Savvas is the protagonist in The Priest's Well.

Spiros (IG) – Naughty boy at the church at the Easter celebrations.

Spiros (BB) – A port police man on Orino Island.

Spiros (TUM) – One of the thugs who abducts Yanni.

Spiros (SB) – Niki's son. Niki is the protagonist in The Stolen Book.

Spiros (RCL) – Vasso's boyfriend, and later husband. He is a driven man, driven to make something of his life but even more driven to provide for those her loves.

Stamatis (RCL) – Spiros's father. Runs the taverna on Orino island. A kindly old man, but in the past he has been too kind and this comes back to cause him problems. Spiros is one of the main characters in The Rush Cutter's Legacy.

Stamos (BB) – A port police man on Orino Island.

Stathis (MPT) – A farmer in the village.

Stathoula (WWB) – Irini's cousin; Glykeria's sister. Irini is the protagonist in Watching the Wind Blow.

Stavros (ENOF, GD, SB) – Stella's husband.

Stefanos (RCL) – A donkey man on Orino island.

Stefi (SB) – Woman behind the counter in George the Greek's café.

Stella (ENOF, GD, MPT, HOP, TUM, WWB, RB, PW, ASATOT, SB, RCL) – Protagonist in The Gypsy's Dream. Runs the eatery / ouzeri in the village, and later builds a hotel on the beach.

Stheno (RB) – Loukas's mother in law who is used to getting her own way. She is sly and sneaky, both of which she believes are ways of being clever. Loukas is the baker in The Reluctant Baker.

Suzi (ABH, TUM) – One of Yanni's donkeys. Yanni is a donkey man on Orino Island.

Takis (TUM) - One of the thugs who abducts Yanni.

Tasso (SB) – Orange buyer who owes Karolos and Niki money. Niki is the protagonist in The Stolen Book.

Terrance (IG, TUM, EL) – Juliet's son, Thomas's twin. Studying waste management at university.

Thanasis (GD, RCL) – Vasso's son, now in Athens.

Thanasis (MPT, TUM, ASATOT) – Donkey breeder in the village.

Themis (ABH) – Dino's father, or at least that is what he would like us to believe!

Themis (SB) – Rich kid, friend of Spiros and Petros. Spiros and Petros are Niki's sons, and Niki is the protagonist in The Stolen Book.

Theo (ENOF, GD, MPT, HOP, TUM, WWB, RB) – The protagonist in In the Shade of the Monkey Puzzle Tree. Manolis' and Mitsos' school friend. Later runs the kafeneio in the village.

Theodoris (RCL)– Spiros' grandfather. Spiros is one of the main characters in The Rush Cutter's Legacy.

Thomas (IG, TUM, EL) – Juliet's son , Terrance's twin. In banking.

Timotheos (MPT) – Baker in Athens who befriends Theo.

Tolis (TUM) - A donkey man on Orino island

Tolis (WWB) – *koulouri* seller. A *koulouri* is a bread ring with sesame seeds eaten all over Greece for breakfast.

Torin (HOP) – Liz's brother. Torin dies in a motorbike accident. Liz is one of the main characters in A Handful of Pebbles.

Toula (EL, SB) – An elderly woman who moved to Saros from the village with her husband Apostolis. Their relationship was good when they first married, but he has withdrawn from her over the years and she feels isolated. Toula is the protagonist in The English Lesson.

Uncle Brian (GD) – Abby's uncle. Has a model train set in the attic.

Vangelis (BB) – Well known Greek composer. Wrote the soundtrack to the film Chariots of Fire.

Vasilis (BB) – A port police man on Orino Island.

Vasilis (RCL) – Leontia's husband. Leontia is an old woman who lives in a village on the mainland, and taught Spiros how to cook in The Rush Cutter's Legacy.

Vasiliki, often shortened to **Vasso** (IG, ENOF, GD, RCL, MPT, TUM, SB, RCL) – Kiosk owner in the village square. Vasso is the protagonist in The Rush Cutter's Legacy, in which she travels to Orino as a young girl.

Vasso (IG) – Little girl at the church at the Easter celebrations – Spiros' sister.

Vasso Mavromati (BB) – Petta's step mother. Petta is Marina's son.

Vetta (TUM) – Sophia's sister, who started a lace making business and did not marry. Sophia is one of the main characters in The Unquiet Mind.

Vlassis (RB) – Assistant deputy planning officer in the town hall in Saros.

Widow Katerina (ENOF) – Village busybody who organized supplies of food for Marina and Mitsos when they were incapacitated after the storm in The Explosive Nature of Friendship.

William (ABH) – Michelle's colleague at the law firm in Bradford where she first worked in law.

Yanni (BB, ABH, TUM) – Donkey man on Orino island. Known as Black Yanni because of his permanent suntan. Yanni is the protagonist in The Unquiet Mind.

Yanni (MPT) – Theo's baba, who is an old man. He ran the kafeneio in the village before passing it on to Theo in In the Shade of the Monkey Puzzle Tree.

Yianni (EL, SB) – A taxi driver in the village.

Yiannis (GD) – Owns the Malibu bar where Jackie is working, and where Abby was hoping to spend the summer.

Yorgos (ASATOT) – A villager.

Yorgos (SB) – An accountant.

Zahari (ABH) – Dino's childhood friend. 'Zahari' literally means 'sugar', and is a nickname derived from the fact that he is diabetic.

Zephyria (EL) – A woman who lives in the village. A friend of Toula's.

Zoe (SB) – Girl in an estate agency office in the UK.

Zorbas (ENOF) – Leni's grandfather. Leni is Mitsos's sister in law.

Good reviews are important to a book's success and will help others find *A Wander Through the Village*. If you enjoyed it, please be kind and leave a review wherever you purchased the book, or on Goodreads.com.

I'm always delighted to receive email from readers, and I welcome new friends on Facebook.

Facebook: https://www.facebook.com/authorsaraalexi

Email: saraalexi@me.com

Happy reading,

Sara Alexi

Also by Sara Alexi

Black Butterflies

The Explosive Nature of Friendship

The Gypsy's Dream

The Art of Becoming Homeless

In the Shade of the Monkey Puzzle Tree

A Handful of Pebbles

The Unquiet Mind

Watching the Wind Blow

The Reluctant Baker

The English Lesson

The Priest's Well

A Song Amongst the Orange Trees

The Stolen Book

The Rush Cutter's Legacy

Saving Septic Cyril : The Illegal Gardener Part II

PUBLISHED BY:

Oneiro Press

The Illegal Gardener

Book One of the Greek Village Collection

28188147R00211

Printed in Poland
by Amazon Fulfillment
Poland Sp. z o.o., Wrocław